Mr. McGregor dropped his hand over hers.

It was warm and alive but he knew he had lost her. The change was final; it had come over her immediately after the accident, a remoteness, a shut door behind her eyes.

She would sit in the kitchen all day, plugging and unplugging the toaster. Norman would yell at her, and she wouldn't have the slightest idea why he was angry. Sometimes she went to the children's room and stood at the window for hours, waiting for them to come home.

"I'm knitting a sweater for Ruthie," she said. "It gets cold at night, and she'll need one."

The old man gripped her hand tighter. Her voice was so calm and confident that he could almost share her fantasy.

Perhaps it *was* real. . . .

PART ONE

The Children

"How doth the little crocodile
  Improve his shining tail,
And pour the waters of the Nile
  On every golden scale!

How cheerfully he seems to grin,
  How neatly spreads his claws,
And welcomes little fishes in,
  With gently smiling jaws!"

—*Alice's Adventures in Wonderland*

The PLAYHOUSE

The PLAYHOUSE

Richard Levinson and William Link

CHARTER BOOKS, NEW YORK

THE PLAYHOUSE

A Charter Book/published by arrangement with
the authors

PRINTING HISTORY
Charter edition/September 1985

Copyright © 1985 by William Link and Richard Levinson

ISBN: 0-441-67071-7

Charter Books are published by The Berkley Publishing Group,
200 Madison Avenue, New York, New York 10016.
PRINTED IN THE UNITED STATES OF AMERICA

Hand over hand, Mr. McGregor climbed clear to the top of the jungle gym, the wind piping in his ears. Behind him surged the children, scrambling up the smooth rungs like monkeys, their heads bobbing against the school yard sky. They whooped and yelled, and Mr. McGregor frolicked above them, then hung from his old legs. Swinging back and forth, his big bat ears red with wind, he felt his pockets pour open and heard coins splashing on the concrete miles below. He took a rusty harmonica from his coat and blew "I've Been Working on the Railroad."

The world spun about, gloriously upside down. "More!" the children shouted, their faces caught in a low-flying cloud. "Play some more!" He started "Oh, Susanna," but the tune froze in his throat. Something was wrong; the jungle gym was beginning to sway. It trembled, tearing loose from its foundations, and suddenly the sky was full of children's screams, streaking orange and red through the sunshine. He tried frantically to catch one of the little girls, but she was out of reach. All around him children were dropping like leaves from a great tree. Down they flew, part of the wind. Soon he was alone, the last leaf, and he could see the children spread over the concrete like his coins.

Mr. McGregor awoke sweating in the dark bedroom. Somewhere, impossibly, a fly was buzzing. It made a thin silver sound.

The old man wiped his face with the sheet. His dream was still fresh, and he pushed his head in his pillow to avoid it, wrapping himself in peaceful memories: his wife on a hammock sipping cider, his daughter's face. Then he remembered the fly.

It was buzzing at the window, and the sound thrilled and revived him. He groped for the control box on the night table, and the bed tilted electronically into a sitting position. The lights went on, picking out the rough Spanish furniture and the aquarium across the room.

Yes! There was the fly, stuck on the pane like a raisin. Mr. McGregor crawled out from under the sheets and tiptoed toward it. Remarkable—a black and delicate thing just like the little wire imitation his grandson Mark had pinned on his coat as a joke. The boy expected to be punished, but Mr. McGregor was delighted; he had even asked him the name of the novelty shop so he could buy another. And now, by some stroke of fortune, there was a real fly in his room, one that he could keep and feed.

Very carefully he closed the blackout curtains, trapping the insect inside. He hurried back to the bed; he'd need an empty matchbox or some kind of small container. There was nothing on the night table except a sticky bottle of cough medicine and his sleeping tablets. He thought of pouring the medicine down the drain and using the bottle, but the fly would be unable to breathe.

Perhaps Billy had a matchbox. He went to the bell-cord beside the bed and gave it a few hard tugs. Then he placed the cold metal of the speaking tube to his ear and listened. No answer. He yanked the cord again, testily, and blew into the tube. "Billy?" he called. "Wake up!"

He glanced at his alarm clock; it was two-thirty in the morning. Could Billy be out of the house? He felt his old heart quicken at the possibility of being alone. When he looked in the bureau mirror a stranger peered out at him, a pale frightened figure with huge ears and dark circles under its eyes. He pressed a trembling finger to the mirror-face to see if it was real and left a gray smear over the nose.

He fled from the reflection, returning to his bed and switching on the hallway lights from the control box. He pushed his soft, blue-veined feet into rope sandals and took a flashlight from the night table drawer. The fish were circling in their aquarium; they peered out at him suspiciously, like the face in the mirror. "Go to sleep," he said. He looked down at his hands. They fluttered ever so slightly, leaves in a wind.

Mr. McGregor left the sanctuary of his bedroom with great trepidation. He didn't trust the house after dark; it threw up objects in his path and made queer sounds. He moved down the hallway, his nightgown slithering behind him on the tile floor. The landing led to the other wing of the large house. A cardboard carton suddenly blocked his way. It was filled with toys—a doll with a face like a sunflower, the snout of a plastic machine gun. Mr. McGregor closed his eyes painfully against the sight of these old relics. Soon they would be moved into the playhouse and shut away.

Downstairs, in the dark living room, the Swiss clock chimed the quarter-hour. The house swallowed the sound.

Mr. McGregor fumbled with the flashlight and clicked it on. The servants' quarters were completely dark. Billy rarely bothered to change the light bulbs after they burned out.

Mr. McGregor started; something wet and warm had brushed his bare leg. He wheeled around, frightened, and pointed the flashlight at the floor. He saw with relief that it was only his cocker spaniel, mooning up at him in the weak rays, the cataracts on both eyes shining like quartz.

"Skipper boy," Mr. McGregor said. He was genuinely glad to see the dog. "Can't you sleep anymore? You're getting as bad as me."

The animal was ancient, its head folded in wrinkles. Confused and half-blind, it roamed the house at night, blundering through the halls or chasing the ghosts of cats in the cellar. Mr. McGregor would usually wake in the mornings and find him curled up on the bed, watching the fish.

"Come along," he said. "Let's see what Billy's up to."

The dog trotted after him to the end of the hallway. The door to Billy's room was closed. A small yellowed bone hung over the frame, an Indian good luck charm. Mr. McGregor eyed it with mistrust; it hinted of witchcraft and voodoo, of dead chickens sprinkled with blood under the moon. He decided he didn't want it in the house any longer. He jiggled it off the ledge, placing it in the pocket of his nightgown. "Billy?"

The door was unlocked. He called the name again, louder, then knocked on one of the panels. "Are you awake?"

He opened the door and beamed the light into the room. Clothes and rum bottles covered the bare floor, glittering like trash in the moonlight. The single bed was a tangle of sleep-tossed sheets and blankets and a few magazines were scattered about, most of them with half-dressed women on their covers. There was little to show that someone lived here. Billy had even taken the pictures from the walls and stacked them in a corner. Skipper nosed through the debris, sniffing at the empty bottles, but Billy was nowhere in sight.

Mr. McGregor couldn't understand it. His heart was beating faster and his breathing was as heavy as the dog's. He turned on the dusty ceiling light but its harsh brightness didn't bring Billy back. There was a mirror near the bed, and he was tempted to look at the stranger with the gray, early-morning face. Instead, he sank down heavily in the room's one chair, deeply afraid.

Dead leaves swirled in the road as Billy Easter came charging up St. Cloud Road on his way to the house. His mouth was open, sucking air, and his shirttail streamed behind him. He was a towering black man with an amiable face and the hands of a basketball player. He lurched slightly as he ran; he had had too much to drink, and he could smell the sour beer in his perspiration.

Each night Billy Easter left the estate to see his woman. This evening they had fought bitterly, and she had dropped him off at the foot of the hill, telling him to get home by himself. He cursed her under his breath. She was getting as crazy as McGregor, but at least she wasn't possessed. The old man was a different story; there were devils poking around inside his head.

He ran faster, kicking at the leaves, his mind spinning with alcohol and speed. Why was he even coming back? Hell, if he had any sense he'd turn around, hitchhike home, and probably catch his fat-ass woman in bed with another man. Then he'd beat her good; he'd make her walk around on her hands and knees like Skipper and then love her up till Mr. Sun stuck his face in the window.

He reached the chain-metal fence and leaned against it, knowing he was safe. He laughed aloud and butted his head at the links. Go to hell police, he thought. He knew all about the special Beverly Hills patrol. They'd just love to pick up a drunken black man and shove him down in the hole to dry out. But he was too smart for them. Go to hell fat cops in your souped-up cars—this boy dances all around you, and you don't see him for dust.

He staggered along the fence, humming to himself, until he came to the red bandana tied around one of the links. Underneath was the opening, and he flopped down and laughed into the earth. What a joke on old McGregor, thinking he was all tucked up in bed, or checking the doors and windows like a night watchman in a bank. He'd never know about the secret tunnel Billy Easter had dug a few weeks before so he could go and sleep with his woman.

Crazy in the head! he thought. That old man should be locked in a closet with cotton stuffed in his ears. The cotton would keep the devils from jumping out and infecting somebody else, especially Billy Easter. But he wasn't worried; he had his bone. No matter what happened, they couldn't mess with that. Go to hell, devils.

He crawled into the little opening and burrowed in the dirt. There was baby, all cool and fine! He unscrewed the cap of the rum bottle and took a long, deep swallow. The liquor burned his tongue, but it was so good he had some more, then he returned his treasure to the dirt. Deeper down, where the bugs couldn't get at it, he had some money buried in an old coin purse he had found in the attic. Some day when he was finished with his woman he would jump a boat back to Jamaica. He would get himself a tourist shop, a candy-striped hut with a tin roof and a sign that said: BILLY EASTER—STRAW HATS—LADIES HAND-BAGS. He would sit on a keg of rum and watch all that money flowing down the pier.

Laughing, his clothing streaked with dirt, he crawled up on the other side of the fence and loped through the knee-high grass. The shrubbery around the house had grown wild and predatory. Rotting plants snared his feet and vines dangled like strings from an old guitar. Billy Easter stumbled, fell, picked himself up, and ran on. He had almost reached the front door when he looked up and saw the ominous light burning in his room.

Mr. McGregor sat brooding in the chair. His hand was pressed against his heart, and he fancied he could feel the movement of his blood. Skipper picked among the bottles, his bright tongue exploring the sugary corks.

The old man was positive he had been deserted. First his wife, his grandchildren, then his daughter—and now Billy. He could cope with loneliness during the long days, but the nights tormented him. Lately, standing at the bedroom window, he had begun to see little faces like strange flowers staring in at him from beyond the fence. He knew they wanted to enter the house so he had taken to locking the gate and sleeping with the key on a shoestring around his neck. Perhaps they were cold out there, and all they wanted was a warm bed, but he couldn't be sure. They made a funny sound, a low humming like electricity and crickets.

Skipper suddenly raised his head, the old ears sweeping back.

"What is it, Skipper boy?" Mr. McGregor asked.

The animal ran over to the open window and stretched its forepaws on the sill.

"Somebody out there?" He could feel the white hairs at the back of his neck begin to lift.

The dog growled. Mr. McGregor realized that he would have to go to the window. The faces would be there, he knew that. Yet it was strange—Skipper had never noticed them before. Perhaps they had managed to get through the fence and come right up to the house. He moved slowly to the window, his eyes half-closed. He promised himself he wouldn't look at them directly, just through the curtains of his lowered lashes.

Someone was standing on the lawn under the window. He stopped squinting and opened his eyes in surprise.

"Hi, there, Mr. McGregor," said Billy Easter. "Who you looking at this time of night?"

The old man gaped at him. "What are you doing out there?" he called angrily. "Where have you been?"

"Long walk. Long, long walk."

"Come up here."

"Throw me a rope. I'll climb right up the side of the house."

Mr. McGregor frowned. "Stop all this foolishness and come up here at once."

Billy ducked through the front door, and the sound of his footfalls charged up the stairs. A moment later he tumbled into the room, a grin on his face. Mr. McGregor was alarmed; the man was covered with loose dirt and smelled of beer. "Settle down," he said uneasily.

Billy Easter's eyes rolled at him. "Don't want to settle down."

Mr. McGregor had never seen him in such a state before; he was actually arrogant. "I want you to go to bed and stop acting like a crazy person."

Billy howled. "You calling *me* crazy? You better get yourself a mirror."

"That's enough."

The black man glared at him defiantly. "Why don't you send for the police?"

"You're being ridiculous."

10

"No, I mean it. Call 'em up and tell them that you lock me in this place at night and don't let me see my woman."

"You get one day off a week. That's perfectly reasonable."

Billy took a step toward him. "You get the police up here, okay? I want 'em to see how you let all those animals run around like a zoo. How you sit in that nightgown all the time and don't even bring any groceries home."

Mr. McGregor retreated. The man was obviously venting grievances he had nursed for months. "You're being unfair, Billy. I always give you plenty to eat."

"You call tuna fish and ice-box cookies *food*? You gonna tell the police you don't have one pound of coffee in this house? About those little *people* you see creepin'. around every night? Man, they'll hang you upside down and stuff olive pits in your mouth."

McGregor sat down on the bed, stung by the man's ingratitude. Hadn't he given Billy some of his old clothes? Didn't he present him with a basket of fruit on Thanksgiving? And now he stood accused of stinginess, of insanity.

Billy Easter was still on the attack. He pointed a finger. "You know where we're going in the morning? Straight to the supermarket. We're gonna load up on some steaks, and a couple quarts of ice cream, and some paper napkins to wipe our mouths with."

"All right, all right," Mr. McGregor mumbled. "Make up a shopping list. We'll buy everything within reason."

"I ain't finished. I want Sunday nights off. If those little *people* show up while I'm not here, well, you just invite them in for a drink." He strutted around the room, vastly pleased with himself. "And I want some furniture in here. I'm getting tired hanging my stuff on the floor." He turned and pointed the finger again. "You listening to all this?"

Mr. McGregor nodded. He felt as if he was being lectured

by a child. Arguments upset him, and he was suddenly exhausted. His eyelids drooped and his right foot had fallen asleep.

"And one of these days I'm gonna want a raise," Billy added. He seemed impressed by his powers of invention.

"Write it all down," said Mr. McGregor. "We'll take care of it in the morning." Absentmindedly, he removed the bone from his pocket and bounced it in his hand. There was a sudden silence. When he looked up he saw that Billy was staring at him, horrified. "What's wrong?" he asked.

"You—got my bone."

"I meant to talk to you about that, Billy. It makes me nervous, sitting up there on your door. Really, it's only a superstition."

The black man didn't say anything.

Mr. McGregor rose from the bed and pocketed the bone. "We both need a good night's sleep," he said. "But I'll be honest with you—you've said some cruel things tonight. I'm willing to let them pass because you're not yourself. In the morning we'll go to the supermarket and pick up those groceries. Is that satisfactory?"

Billy nodded slowly.

Mr. McGregor gave him a worried look, held the door open for Skipper, and closed it gently behind him. The dog nuzzled his leg and lifted its head to be petted. You're the only one I can trust, Mr. McGregor thought with a feeling of regret. Billy was no longer reliable. Eventually he'd have to place an ad in the paper for a new servant-chauffeur, someone older and dependable, a teetotaler. Billy deserved a second chance, a grace period, but it was doubtful that he would change. Damn! he suddenly thought. In all the excitement he had forgotten to get a matchbox for the fly.

He hurried back to his bedroom, praying that nothing had happened, but when he parted the curtains he saw that somehow, mysteriously, the fly had escaped.

12

THE PLAYHOUSE

* * *

Deep in his dream woodpeckers were boring, their sharp beaks splintering wood, sucking up insects. Mr. McGregor woke with a start, listening to the crash of hammers slipping through the blackout curtains.

He sat up in bed. Skipper was lying across his legs, a dead weight. He eased the animal to the floor and went quickly to the window, throwing open the heavy drapes. He looked down majestically from the second story at the playhouse in the backyard. It was almost finished, a bright little boat complete with cabin, captain's bridge, and a gold wooden anchor that floated incongruously in the grass. A group of workmen in overalls moved around the vessel, hammering the roof and fitting glass in the portholes. Mr. McGregor was thrilled; everything looked tidy and ship-shape. Within a few short days it would be complete, ready for its imaginary sea voyage. How did they dedicate new boats—with a crack of champagne across the bow? Perhaps when they picked up Billy's groceries they would also buy some wine.

One of the carpenters, sitting astride the sloping roof, saw him and saluted ironically. He knew he was an object of vast amusement for the workmen; they thought it strange that a childless old man should be erecting a playhouse in his yard. But he never bothered explaining; it was too complicated. He saluted back. No sense being unfriendly. They were professionals, and they had done a fine job, and if they wanted to laugh behind his back it didn't really matter. All that counted was the result of their labors.

Mr. McGregor shaved over an earthenware basin, dressed in a neat blue banker's suit, and went downstairs. The house never frightened him during the day. The rooms were high and spacious, the conquistador ceilings ribbed with rough wooden rafters. The furniture—his wife had purchased most of it in Mexico City—was cheerful and exotic, but there wasn't quite enough of it to fill the rooms with a look of cluttered comfort. Mr. McGregor always intended to buy more but he never seemed to find the time, and now he was frequently aware of the stark and empty corners, the tile corridors that needed carpeting. And the place was disgracefully untended; layers of dust covered every surface and even the plants, his wife's pride and joy, were choking in their clay pots. If Billy wanted concessions, he would have to make a few in return.

Mr. McGregor went into the kitchen and poured milk into pans for the cats. He was slicing a grapefruit for himself when someone knocked on the door.

It was Mr. Leary, the foreman, a rangy man with a blue tattoo on his arm. "Morning," he said.

"Good morning," said Mr. McGregor. "How is everything coming?"

"No problems. We'll be painting in a day or two."

Mr. McGregor could sense the man's curiosity. He probably had an itch to roam through the house and see what it was like, but he had never been beyond the kitchen. His eyes strayed to the cats lapping at their milk, and Mr. McGregor was sure he could read his mind. Cats but no children. Was the playhouse a refuge for animals? Or, did the old man intend to play captain all by himself, dressed up in a tunic with gold braid.

"Is there something I can do for you?"

Mr. Leary shrugged. "Thought you might want to know about your colored boy. When we got here this morning we found him asleep on the boat."

"Billy? In the playhouse?"

"Curled up like a possum. Figured I'd better talk to you before I woke him up."

Mr. McGregor found he was still holding the grapefruit.

He set it down. "Thank you for telling me."

The foreman squinted through the kitchen arch toward the living room. "You live here all alone?" he asked. "I mean, just you and your chauffeur?"

Mr. McGregor didn't answer him. Instead, he strode out on the lawn and up the steps of the playhouse, nodding to the carpenters. The entrance was built like a bridge, with a ship's wheel and a chrome toy barometer.

"Nice day for sailing," said one of the workmen.

"Mmm," Mr. McGregor mumbled, aware that he was being taunted. He entered the playhouse and closed the door so that they couldn't pry. The large, shadowed room was fitted out as a ship's cabin, walled in dark wood and studded with brass. In one corner stood a massive sea chest, its latch securely padlocked. A long marble counter faced by rows of wire stools ran the length of the far wall. It was like an ice cream parlor fountain out of Mr. McGregor's Michigan childhood, and he had decorated it with nickel soda taps, giant apothecary jars, and a heart-shaped mirror that he had unearthed in an antique shop near the ocean. Slumped on one of the stools, his face pressed flat to the marble, was Billy Easter, fast asleep.

Mr. McGregor was shocked. This was a violation. He marched over to Billy and shook him roughly by the shoulder. "Wake up!" he commanded.

Billy jerked away from the marble, his eyes snapping open. He blinked. Then he saw the old man and lurched back.

"You're not supposed to be in here! Do you understand? Why in heaven's name didn't you sleep in your bed?"

Billy looked around the cabin. "Figured I'd get a better rest out here."

"What are you talking about?"

"I don't like my room anymore," Billy said. "That's all. I just don't like it."

Mr. McGregor's voice was firm. "You promised never to come in here without my permission. You broke your word."

The black man yawned, unintimidated. He stretched his arms until his knuckles almost brushed the ceiling. "I'll move into one of the other rooms tonight. Okay?"

"As long as you stay away from here."

"Sure. Right."

Mr. McGregor saw Billy's eyes drift toward the padlocked sea chest. "We're going shopping," he said. "Put on your uniform."

Another yawn. "There's a hole in it."

"Then sew it up. I'm visiting my son-in-law this afternoon."

Billy shrugged, spun around on the stool, and went sulkily to the door. A carpenter looked in one of the portholes, pretending to check the glass.

Mr. McGregor turned away. The room was intended as a shrine, a memorial, and now it had been defiled by Billy's presence and the curious workman at the window. All he wanted was peace and a place of his own to think. It seemed unfair that everywhere he turned the world had its eye at a peephole.

They bought the groceries at a nearby supermarket. Billy filled the shopping cart with steaks and ice cream while the old man waited at the check-out counter, watching little children with their mothers. Some of them had set out on adventures, dazzled by the ripe fruits and the hanging scales of the produce section. Others drew faces on the chill glass of the refrigeration units. He followed them longingly with his eyes, a silent secret partner in their games. When one of the mothers bent down to study a row of cans, he wiggled

16

his fingers at her child in the cart. The baby stared at him with wide, wondering eyes, then it grinned and giggled. Mr. McGregor was pleased.

They left the supermarket and drove through the flat, treeless streets of Santa Monica, where belts of stucco apartment buildings stood on stilts to accommodate garages that smelled of cement. "Want me to go past the school yard?" asked Billy.

"No." Mr. McGregor was reminded of his dream, the flutter of little dresses like handkerchiefs in the wind.

"We're near enough. Just around the block."

"Not today. I want you to take me to the factory."

Billy Easter shrugged and turned the car toward the ocean.

McGREGOR BATHING SUITS, INC. was a few blocks from the beach, a low, pigeon-gray building with a loading ramp jutting from the rear. They wheeled off the street and pulled to a stop by the front entrance doors. A huge billboard looked down at them with a picture of a languid girl lying against a bright green ocean, and the slogan: *"Get in the Swim with McGregor."*

Billy Easter opened the car door, drinking in the long body on the sign.

"Wait for me," Mr. McGregor said.

"Always do."

The old man shuffled into the reception foyer with its glass panel overlooking the main office area. He seldom came to the factory anymore, and when he did he felt like an unwelcome ghost in a house he had no business haunting. There were still faces from the past, people he had hired ten or fifteen years ago, and he dreaded greeting them. It was a terrible effort to remember their names.

The girl at the reception desk was smiling at him. "Mr. McGregor. So nice to see you. I'll tell Mr. Abbott you're here."

He nodded at her mechanically, standing with his back

to the glass so that no one would recognize him. The place smelled the same, a dark odor of paper and rubber.

The girl swung around from her switchboard. "He'll be right with you," she said. "Why don't you take a seat?"

Mr. McGregor sat down on a comfortable leather sofa. I should have told him I was coming, he thought. He could have prepared himself, made excuses.

The muted sound of machinery drifted through the far wall. The assembly area, where the bathing suits were manufactured and packed, occupied the entire rear section of the building. Mr. McGregor remembered the first time he had taken his grandchildren back there—he had waited until they were old enough to appreciate it. Mark had been delighted by the conveyor belt. He had climbed aboard and ridden it between the tables of half-completed suits, shouting as if he were on a horse. Ruthie had been very ladylike, crinkling her nose and pointing a delicate finger. "Make him stop, Granddad," she had said. "He'll hurt himself."

Norman came into the reception foyer. His shirtsleeves were rolled to the elbows, exposing his thick forearms. He seemed mildly annoyed, as if he had been swept away from an important call or a new pattern on the drawing board. "Dad," he said. "Why didn't you tell me you were coming?"

"I thought I'd surprise you."

Norman nodded, as if he expected this, and held open a side door that led to his office. Mr. McGregor noticed with apprehension that though the room was physically the same, all the furnishings had been changed. Draperies screened the noon light and a stark Danish desk, empty except for a bouquet of pencils in a jar, stood under a lamp that raised and lowered at a touch. He thought of his old desk, bulky and huge and heaped with reports.

"Sit down, sit down," Norman said, rolling his sleeves another notch above the elbows. "How have you been?"

"Fine."

"How's Billy?"

"Fine."

Norman dropped down into the chair behind the desk. With his usual questions gone he seemed at a loss, ready to terminate the interview. "It's funny," he said at length, not meeting the old man's eyes, "I was going to call you this morning."

A lie, Mr. McGregor thought. He looked at two framed photographs on a table by the window. One showed a pretty woman with wings of glossy dark hair—Norman's new wife. The other was of a baby sitting up in a bassinet, thrusting a spoon at the camera. For a moment he was glad that everything had turned out well for Norman. He really wasn't a bad person. Caught up with himself, perhaps, overly involved with his own needs and problems, but he had made his daughter a decent husband.

"Matter of fact, I even jotted down a note to remind me," Norman continued, a little guiltily. "See. Right here on the pad."

Mr. McGregor glanced at it, not really interested. It said: *Dad. Picnic.*

"I'm throwing a shindig for the staff on Saturday," Norman explained, as if he was relieved that he had established something concrete between them. "Beer, cold cuts— full day's outing. Why don't you drop by? They'll be glad to see you."

"It might be awkward," Mr. McGregor said.

"Don't be foolish. What happened, happened. Water under the bridge."

"Saturday's a bad day."

Norman waved an impatient hand. "No excuses." He paused, then placed both elbows on the desktop. "You know, sometimes I worry about you up there in that place. No one to look after you except that ridiculous chauffeur. You're like a hermit."

You could invite me for dinner once in a while, he thought with a surge of bitterness. Introduce me to your wife, let me play with your new baby. But you're afraid, especially because of the child. And I really can't blame you. "I'm used to it," he said.

"Yeah, but you should get out of that house now and then. Take in a few movies."

Mr. McGregor wanted to change the subject. "How's your family?" he asked.

"Okay," said Norman after a moment's hesitation. "The baby was just three yesterday, we had a little party."

A light flashed on a box behind him. Gratefully, he picked up the phone. "Yes? . . . Tell them I'll be right out." He stood up and moved around the desk, safely back in the embrace of his business. "That was Ollie. They're having trouble with the motor on the belt."

Mr. McGregor took his cue, rose from the chair.

Norman dropped an arm over his shoulder. "Hang around, we'll have some coffee later."

"No, I have an errand."

"Don't forget Saturday. You'll have a ball. We're going to shoot off fireworks after dark."

"I'll see if I can rearrange my schedule."

"Schedule?" Norman laughed. "Hell, that was when you ran this nightmare of a place. Take it easy for a change. Sell that witch's castle of yours and go to Palm Springs."

He guided the old man out of the office and into the reception foyer. "Listen," he said, his voice low and confidential, "I've been meaning to go up and see Loretta, but it's been impossible around here. I honestly haven't had a chance to get away. If you see her, tell her I'll drop by as soon as I can."

"Of course."

Norman squeezed his arm. "Good. And don't forget about Saturday. I want you there, okay?"

The limousine climbed along the hillside. Far below, surfers rode the waves into the crowded beach. The air was smoky; somewhere, back in the hills, a forest fire was burning. Mr. McGregor could see two single-engine planes swooping low in the sky. They would probably find the flames and drop chemicals.

At the crest of the hill a small clearing, much like a private park, had been cut from the trees, and men in T-shirts rode mechanized lawn mowers through the grass. Perched over the Pacific was a great wooden house, ringed by a moat of azaleas. It was painted gray, like a military installation, and its television antenna drooped with gulls. There was a long, precarious porch where people in sunglasses sat watching the water.

Billy stopped the car in the parking lot, slid a piece of gum in his mouth, and opened a newspaper to the horoscope section.

"You ought to walk around and get some air in your lungs," Mr. McGregor said, climbing out of the car. He instantly regretted the remark—it sounded too much like Norman with his pocketful of panaceas. "I won't be long," he added.

A Good Humor man was selling ice cream to some children on the front lawn. Mr. McGregor paused and watched the scene. He felt like treating them, a generous stranger they would remember for weeks. But he decided against it and climbed the steps.

The lobby was a big, booming room with a wooden staircase leading up to the wards and recreation areas. Patients strolled about aimlessly, and visitors sat on overstuffed couches, their hands hidden by flowers. At the desk a nurse was smoking a cigarette. She stubbed it out as Mr. McGregor approached.

"Is Mrs. Loretta Abbott available?" he asked in a hushed voice. The visits always made him feel like a stranger in a church of another faith.

The nurse consulted a file and then picked up the desk phone. "Who's calling?"

"Her father."

She talked briefly with someone named Stauderman, then replaced the receiver. "It's all right. The third floor, all the way in the back. Do you know where it is?"

Mr. McGregor nodded. He preferred the stairway, but it required too much exertion to climb the three long flights. The elevator frightened him; a cramped steel box with a droning fan. Today it was filled with well-dressed women, their faces set in grave, hospital expressions. Someone, probably a child, had let a balloon loose, and it drifted along the ceiling looking down at them.

Mr. McGregor, pushed to the rear, stared at the dust on the tips of his shoes. They were nearing the second floor, and he felt an oppressive, restless sensation in his chest. It always came over him when he visited his daughter, and it would leave as soon as he left the building and walked out under the bright sky and the dipping gulls.

The elevator dropped him on the third floor, and he moved quickly down the corridor, his eyes straight ahead, not wanting to see the prowling patients who sometimes popped out at him and started elaborate conversations. He knocked on the door of 327 and went in.

Loretta sat on the edge of the bed watching a television set. She looked up at him calmly, then turned back to the screen. The curtains were drawn against the daylight, and the room was filled with a blurred orange haze like the azaleas outside. "Loretta?" he said. "It's Dad."

"Hello." Her eyes were still on the screen. A cartoon flickered, foxes talking to ducks.

Mr. McGregor groped his way across the room and sat down on the bed beside her. She was wearing a cocktail dress and a single strand of pearls at her throat. She might have been waiting for Norman to finish dressing on their way to a restaurant. "How have you been?" he asked.

"All right." The television light broke now and then across her thin face. She looked young, not like a woman of thirty-five who had raised a son and daughter and managed a household. There was a quality of extreme trust in her expression, and he felt like slipping her onto his lap, stroking the dark hair and placing a spoon between her fingers.

"I was going to bring you flowers," he said, "but I thought maybe you were tired of them."

"I am," she said. "Norman sent me some last week. Roses."

"I just saw him. He said he'll drive up to see you soon."

"That's nice." She pressed a button on the remote control box, and the set switched to a movie.

Mr. McGregor looked away from her face to the screen. The sound was low, and there was something soothing about the gray images. He found himself thinking of all of them, Mark and Ruthie included, waiting in the living room while the smell of his wife's cooking curled from the kitchen. Norman would be home at six with a new toy for the children, a tin monkey that ate pennies and tapped a drum.

Loretta lay back on the bed, her head touching the wall. She folded her hands and closed her eyes.

"Loretta," he said softly, "do you want to sleep?"

"No."

"Can we talk?"

She nodded drowsily. "How's Mark doing at school?"

23

Mr. McGregor was at a loss. The doctor had warned him about these lapses and told him to ignore them. But he couldn't play games with his own daughter; he believed that in some vague way he could help her. "Mark is gone," he said honestly.

"I don't think his teacher likes him," said Loretta. "He's much too bright for the rest of the class."

Mr. McGregor dropped his hand over hers. It was warm and alive but he knew that he had lost her. The change was final; it had come over her immediately after the accident, a remoteness, a shut door behind her eyes. She would sit in the kitchen all day, plugging and unplugging the toaster. Norman would yell at her, and she wouldn't have the slightest idea why he was angry. Sometimes she went up to the children's room and stood for hours at the window, waiting for them to come running up the lawn.

"I'm knitting a sweater for Ruthie," she said. "It gets cold at night, and she'll need one."

The old man gripped her hand tighter. Her voice was so calm and confident that he could almost share her fantasy. Here in the dark room with the silent set, away from his house and Norman, he had the queer feeling that what she was saying was true. Mark and Ruthie had gone to camp. They were across the water on Catalina Island, and they were both playing at this very moment in their summer bunks. In a few days Billy would drive him to the pier where they would be waiting in their white camp uniforms, their brown arms hugging handicraft gifts for Mommy and Daddy and Granddad.

Perhaps it *was* real. This was a resort hotel, Loretta was taking a summer vacation herself. He'd pack her clothes, pay the bill, and have the car brought around. He could hear himself telling the other guests that she was going home to her husband and children.

There was a light tapping on the door. Mr. McGregor

released his daughter's hand. A moment later the door opened and a young doctor looked in. "Oh," he said, smiling at the old man. "You must be Loretta's father. I'm new here, Dr. Stauderman."

Mr. McGregor rose and shook hands. He wondered if the doctor could tell what he had been thinking.

"No lights again, Loretta?" the man said, gently scolding. "You're going to save us a fortune on the electric bill."

. Loretta didn't seem to hear; she was still reclining on the bed, her fingers linked, her newly enameled nails shining.

"Mad at me today?" Dr. Stauderman asked.

"No. I was talking to my father."

"You go right ahead. I just wanted to meet him."

Loretta sighed. "We don't have much to say."

Mr. McGregor looked warily at the doctor who was smiling at him for no apparent reason. He didn't care for this new man; he seemed the type who would discuss his patients with the pretty nurses during coffee breaks.

"I was going to show him the sweater I'm knitting for Ruthie," Loretta said. "He didn't seem very interested."

"Where is it?" Dr. Stauderman asked pleasantly.

"In the drawer."

"We'd both like to see it. Why don't you get up and show it to us?"

Loretta turned her face to the wall. "No," she said.

Dr. Stauderman snapped off the television set. "Are you sleepy, Loretta? You look sleepy to me."

"A little."

"Did you eat your lunch this afternoon?"

"Just the creamed corn."

"Why don't we get you your milk shake?" He turned to the old man. "Your daughter likes a milk shake in the afternoon."

"Strawberry this time," said Loretta.

25

"And try to get some rest while we're gone. Mrs. Frasier told me you hardly slept at all last night."

"I don't like to sleep."

Mr. McGregor swallowed; the uneasy feeling was still with him. "Honey," he said, "you rest. I'll be back some other time."

"But you just came," she pouted. She suddenly reminded him of Ruthie, querulous and anxious at bedtime.

"You really should get some sleep. I'm sure Dr. Stauderman knows best."

She was silent. Mr. McGregor bent over the bed and kissed her lightly on the hair. A vase of artificial flowers stood on the night table beside her. Somehow, impossibly, the bouquet seemed to be shedding; tiny dried blossoms had come loose and dotted the tabletop like crumbs. He kissed her again, this time on the forehead, and followed the doctor to the door.

"When you come again, I want you to bring me something," Loretta said.

"Of course. What would you like?"

"I need some wool. Navy blue. You can buy it in that little shop in Westwood."

"He won't forget," Dr. Stauderman interjected. "Now suppose we get some sleep."

As the door closed behind them Mr. McGregor felt a swell of relief. He noticed that the doctor was no longer cheerful; he had left his smile in the room.

They walked toward the elevator and Stauderman said, "How often do you visit her?"

"I try to see her once a week. Something like that."

"Perhaps you should come less frequently."

There was something suspicious in the man's face, something that reminded Mr. McGregor of Norman. "My daughter expects me. She *likes* to see me."

"I'm sure she does. But you stir certain memories. They can disturb her if we're not careful."

"I'm her father," he grumbled. "In fact, I've been thinking that one of these days I could take her out for a ride. She looks so pale, never any sun. I have a car and a chauffeur, it wouldn't be much trouble. . . ."

They had reached the elevator. Dr. Stauderman stood mulling it over, his hands on his hips. "It's a possibility," he said finally. The smile reappeared, disarming and friendly. "You live with your son-in-law now?"

"No. I live by myself."

"Mmmm." More thinking. "Well—maybe both of you could take her for a drive one of these days." He held out his hand. "Nice meeting you, Mr. McGregor. Let's get together for a chat soon."

Mr. McGregor took the hand but avoided the eyes. It was Norman looking at him, a younger Norman, with the same unstated accusation. He wondered if the doctor had children.

The elevator arrived, and Stauderman clapped him on the back. Then the door closed and he could hardly wait until he reached the lobby. He knew he wouldn't bring Loretta the wool; he wanted to take her something better, a gift, and it should be out of the ordinary. Not flowers, nor clothing, nor even a book. It had to be unique, something that would tie them together again and let her know he was sorry.

The doors slid open. Still pondering, Mr. McGregor hurried toward the blinding rim of sky at the entrance. He could already feel the warm air. A gift for Loretta. He would have to think about it.

* * *

On Saturday Mr. McGregor rose at a reasonable hour and inspected the finished playhouse. It had been painted the previous afternoon, oyster-white and royal-blue, and the colors were still wet in the fresh light of morning. The old man calculated that it would be dry by evening, and he could begin moving the children's toys inside.

"Mr. McGregor," Billy Easter called from the kitchen. "Telephone."

It was Norman, his voice buoyant and friendly. "Well? Are you coming?"

Mr. McGregor hesitated. The world was crowding in on him. There was moving to be done, a gift to consider for his daughter, and now here was Norman trying to involve him in a picnic. "I have some errands," he said.

"No excuses. You want to sit in that house all day and count your toes? Come on. At least put in an appearance."

"Well . . ." Mr. McGregor sighed.

"Seriously, Dad, you might enjoy it."

The old man glanced through a window at the sky. It was a lovely day, cloudless, with puffs of bright wind from the ocean. "Where's it going to be?" he said finally.

"Same as always, the lake. Hell, you were the one who started these things."

Mr. McGregor remembered the picnics of the past. They were usually held in the fall, with a rented bus to pick up the employees from their scattered homes. Ruthie would always manage to be stung by a bee, and he'd fix a poultice of mud on her arm to soothe the irritation. She'd cry herself to sleep in the shade while her brother lit firecrackers and frightened the other children. "They seem so long ago," he admitted, thinking of the vanished autumn lake and the couples in canoes.

"Come anytime after one. We'll be expecting you."

"I'll be there." He slowly hung up the phone.

Billy Easter was sitting at the kitchen table, picking at a plate of scrambled eggs and bacon.

"We're going to a picnic," the old man announced.

"Wet or dry?"

"If I know my son-in-law, he'll have kegs of cold beer."

"Then I'd better wash the car," Billy Easter grinned.

It was just as Mr. McGregor remembered it; nothing had changed except for a few signs warning of littering and the floating fumes of gasoline from private boats cruising the lake. Even the diving board seemed the same, a rotting plank matted with algae, where a small boy stood making faces for his father's camera.

The old man looked around the buzzing picnic hollow with surprise and a touch of envy. Dozens of families were gathered on the hot grass, some lolling on crazy-quilt blankets, others lined up for the simmering hamburgers on the portable barbecue grills. Norman must have doubled the staff, Mr. McGregor speculated, or else there were gate crashers. The men congregated at the beer kegs, moving off gingerly with foaming cups toward their picnic plots. Everyone had staked off a square of sunlight, and the children courted poison ivy in the bushes or shouted up at a skywriting plane that was scrawling a message over the lake.

"Mr. McGregor?" a voice said hesitantly.

The old man turned, vaguely intimidated. Here was a face he should remember, a wry, wrinkled face with a blue baseball cap pulled down over gray hair. "I don't believe—" he began.

"Fred Schalkenbach," the man reminded him, a bit disappointed. "Night watchman at the plant?" he added.

"Oh yes, yes," Mr. McGregor said. The baseball cap

and the gaudy sportshirt had distracted from a face he should have recognized. "How have you been. Schalkenbach?"

"So-so. They're putting me out to pasture next year. Twenty-two years at the plant. Guess nobody can beat that record except you."

Mr. McGregor smiled sadly. He liked this old man; once they had shared a few drinks at the factory after an emergency night fire. "They put me out to pasture, too. How are things going?"

"Same. Pretty quiet. Sometimes we get teenagers, like to drive their cars on the lot and do some smooching. No trouble, though. I just give 'em the flashlight." He laughed and moved closer, his voice confidential. "You should see the new uniform your son-in-law makes me wear. My wife says I look like a marine without the medals. Security police officer—that's what Mr. Abbott calls me.

"Twenty-two years," Mr. McGregor reflected. "You must have come just after we started."

"Almost the very beginning," said Schalkenbach proudly. "Long time ago. What are you doing now? Taking it easy?"

"Taking it easy." He was sure Schalkenbach must have heard about the accident; there had been rumors all over the factory. He held out his hand. "Well, I'll see you around."

The night watchman smiled. "No friends like the old friends."

Mr. McGregor moved away. He would have to put in a good word with Norman. If Schalkenbach was retiring they should give him a dinner, an extra bonus for his years of loyalty.

Norman was cooking steaks on the grill, his face wet with smoke. "Dad!" he exclaimed. "Glad you came."

"I said I would, didn't I?"

The younger man handed him a plate heaped with meat and a mountain of potato salad. "What a victory. Never

30

thought I'd get you out of that house. You want some mustard?"

"No, thank you." He looked at the steak; he wasn't really hungry.

"I want you to meet Sharon and the baby," said Norman, loading more plates and handing them out, "Sharon!" he called off toward the trees. No one answered. "She's probably got the radio on. Why don't you go over and introduce yourself? They're right behind that table over there. Wait— don't you want some coffee?"

Mr. McGregor stood patiently while his son-in-law poured. He didn't want to meet Sharon and the child.

"Right over there," said Norman. "You can see her head."

The old man couldn't delay any longer. He nodded and went off in the direction of the wooden table, balancing his plate on the coffee cup. Why hadn't Norman left him alone? It would have been a pleasant enough afternoon stretched in the shade, watching the children play their games. But he had to admit to himself that he was curious, and soon he had stopped near the table and was looking through the screen of bushes.

A lush young woman lay on a blanket with the cord of a Walkman plugged in her ear. She was dark and pretty— prettier than Loretta he noted with a touch of resentment, her young legs casually displayed in shorts. She seemed committed to the radio, bored with the picnic and her baby. The child lay next to her on the blanket, looking up at the sky through the trees. It resembled Norman, just as Mark and Ruthie had. He was suddenly angry at the child and even angrier at Norman for remarrying. But the feeling quickly passed. It was his own fault, after all.

He moved off before the woman saw him. It would have been impossible to introduce himself. (Hello, I'm Mr. McGregor, Norman's ex-father-in-law.) He could imagine the frightened look in her eyes; her hand would reach out for the baby. No, he would never meet them, and it was just as well.

A game of baseball was starting. Sides were being chosen and sluggish, indoor fathers were peeling off shirts, using some of the garments for base markers. Billy Easter was with them, a cup of beer in one hand, a fielder's glove in the other. Over the lake, the plane had finished its message: WELCOME MCGREGOR PICNIC in tall, chalky letters that were already beginning to fade. The old man smiled. Norman was giving them quite a show. He knew that Loretta would have been dazzled. But the new Mrs. Abbott hadn't even noticed; she was too busy with her radio and her sunbathing.

Mr. McGregor felt exhausted. He sat down at the base of a tree and opened his napkin, spreading it over his face. He closed his eyes and listened to the soft, far-off sounds of the ball game, the buzz of motorboats on the lake. Even through the napkin he could feel the sun on his old face, pressing warm thumbs on his eyelids. He heard Billy Easter's voice coming down a long tunnel like a train: "Cover that man on second!" Drowsing, he was glad that Norman's picnic was a success. . . .

Mr. McGregor's eyes snapped open. A breeze off the lake had shifted the napkin down over his nose. Someone was standing close by, watching him. He peeked and saw two little brown legs, white cotton socks. He looked up, uneasily, into a child's face, and found himself staring into the enormous blue eyes of Ruthie. He wanted to cry out her name, shout for Norman to come and see. But the little girl wasn't his grandchild; she resembled Ruthie only slightly with her long taffy hair and sweetly upturned nose. Why had he been so shocked, so mistaken? He studied her face and the way she held herself. There was something of Ruthie's demeanor about her, a cool and detached pride that had always made him suspect there was an adult hidden in her child's body.

"Look!" the little girl said. She thrust out her arm, showing him a tiny cut like a drop of red wax on her elbow. "I fell." The muscles around her eyes bunched, but she seemed to exert a discipline that held the tears in check.

Mr. McGregor was unable to speak. She's not Ruthie, he told himself sharply. She belongs to someone else.

She blinked several times, but her face remained serene. "Should I put a leaf on it?" she asked.

"No," he said. "No, don't do that." Ruthie with her annual bee sting, holding back the tears so her brother wouldn't see. And he would shape a little cake of mud and place it tenderly on the pain. "Where are your mommy and daddy?" he asked.

The little girl didn't answer; she was staring past him, beyond the tree, toward some distant region in the bushes. The grass rustled, and Mr. McGregor turned his head to see what had drawn her attention.

Mark was creeping out from the trees. It *was* Mark, a dark, tense little boy with curly black hair and funny flat ears pressed close to his head.

Mr. McGregor clutched the trunk of the tree, deeply frightened. The boy was still advancing, crawling like an animal on his hands and knees. Mark. The name almost escaped from his mouth. Loretta was right; it was a mistake, a dream.

"Hi," the boy said to the little girl. "Haven't you seen a dog before?"

"You're *not* a dog," the girl said.

Mr. McGregor looked down into the child's small sly

face. No, it wasn't Mark after all. Another mistake his eyes had played on him. There was a faint echo, a dim resemblance, but this was an ugly boy with narrow eyes and a greedy mouth. It was Mark after a school yard fight, his features exaggerated and flushed with anger.

The boy rolled over on his back, like Skipper. "What did you do to your arm?" he asked. He seemed pleased with his new vantage point.

"I fell." She cupped her hand over the cut so he couldn't see it.

"You're going to get a big sore," he said.

"No, I'm not."

"Yes you are. It's going to spread all over your arm right down to your fingers."

The girl seemed puzzled. "It won't."

"Yes, it will. And then your whole arm is going to drop off, and we'll have to put it in a box and bury it."

"You're stupid," she said, but she peeked at the cut to see if it was spreading.

Mr. McGregor didn't move. He stood watching the teasing contest, totally absorbed. They were like Mark and Ruthie at bedtime, picking at each other in an elaborate ritual. He almost felt as if he didn't exist. The little girl had completely forgotten him and the boy had never acknowledged his presence.

The boy was smiling now. "You're scared," he said. "You can't jump rope with only one arm."

"I'll grow another one."

"I think I'll tell Mom you cut yourself."

"Don't."

"I think I will." He sprang to his feet and reached for her arm. The little girl's tears finally broke; she tried to push back at him, but he darted nimbly away. "I'm going to tell Mom!" he sang joyously.

The girl chased after him, crying openly now, as he tore

across the clearing and headed for a cluster of blankets around the ball game. Mr. McGregor watched them run, breathing along with them as if he were racing himself. At a distance they were exactly like his grandchildren, dodging about his back lawn in a forgotten twilight. Before he quite realized it, he was following after them.

"Watch out for the ball!" Billy Easter shouted.

Something white, a piece of the sun, exploded on his head. The world went dizzy for a moment, and he felt grass in his mouth. There were ants in the grass, tickling his tongue.

"You all right?" Billy Easter asked, genuinely concerned.

Mr. McGregor groaned. He was lying on his face on the lawn. The ground trembled beneath him as people came running up.

"Are you okay?" Billy asked again. He bent over, his body blocking the sun.

Things were growing clearer now. He sat up and touched his head, looking around at trousers and bare legs. "Knocked the wind out of me," he said, coughing and spitting grass.

"Somebody get a doctor," shouted a voice.

"From where?" came the answer. "There's no doctor around here."

The old man sat hugging his knees. He was suddenly very cold. The back of his head felt white hot, as if the sun had found a chink in the crowd and was training its rays on the bump. His eyes had a queer double vision, multiplying all the legs and running the colors together. For a moment he thought he saw the sly littly boy observing him—two little boys, their Siamese faces bleeding away from each other like cells under a microscope.

"Let's break this up, give him some air." It was Norman's authoritative voice.

The crowd moved away, and he was sitting again in a hot pool of sunlight.

"You feel all right?" Norman asked.

Something clicked in his brain, and his normal vision returned. "I think so."

"Let's see that bump." Norman brushed grass from the hair and touched the swelling skin. "That's a real beauty."

"He walked right into the ball," said Billy Easter, as if it were his duty to apologize. "I shouted at him, but it was too late."

"Better take him home," said Norman. "Get some cold compresses on that lump. Can you stand up, Dad?"

The old man made an effort to rise, and Billy caught him under the armpits.

"I'm—fine," Mr. McGregor said. His ears had been ringing, but now they cleared, and he could hear the sounds of children and the crack of the baseball bat again. Norman and Billy helped him across the lawn to his car. His legs were unsteady, but he was sure everything would be fine if he could get out of the sun.

"Better call a doctor when you get home," Norman instructed Billy. "I wouldn't take a chance on something like this. He's not a young kid anymore."

When they reached the car, Mr. McGregor swayed against the hood, getting his breath.

"Want some ice cream, Dad? Something cold?"

"No. No thanks."

Billy Easter helped him gently into the back seat. Norman took a cushion and propped it under his head. "Sorry this had to happen," he said. "I wanted you to stay for supper and watch the fireworks."

"It's all right, Norman. I had a good time anyway." He smiled reassuringly.

"Promise me you'll send for a doctor."

"Yes." Norman was always extracting promises. Why couldn't he trust him once in a while?

"Call me if you need anything."

Mr. McGregor wasn't listening. His eyes were fixed on the path that led through the forest to the lake. The two children were prancing along it, perfect friends again, both of them sucking on popsicles. A slim blonde woman was behind them, probably their mother. She wore tight denim shorts, and her hair was in a ponytail like a teenager's. "That woman," he said to Norman. "Right over there. Does she work at the plant?"

"In the packing room. Why?"

"No special reason. I—saw her before at the game. She didn't seem to be enjoying herself."

Norman shrugged. "Look, all I provide is the beer and the lake. Who can please everybody?"

"What's her name?" he asked offhandedly.

"Hubbard." Norman seemed bored. He had performed his duty and issued his instructions. "If you need anything, call," he said.

Mr. McGregor nodded, watching the children as they ran, soaring, deep into the afternoon. Mark and Ruthie on a Saturday picnic. They were blurred now, hazy. His head ached.

Billy Easter started the car, and Norman leaned at the window. "Hope you *did* have a good time," he said, almost as if he doubted it. "See anyone from the old days?"

"Yes," he said wearily, resting his head on the cushion. "From the old days."

Mr. McGregor did not call a doctor. He lay like a dead man on his bed while Billy Easter brought clean linen handkerchiefs and soup bowls filled with ice cubes. He bathed his head a few times and then grew bored, flicked the lights on and off from the control box.

"Norman said I should get a doctor," Billy reminded him.

"I don't need one."

"Suppose you die up here in the middle of the night? What's supposed to happen then?"

"You have a terrible imagination. I'm not going to die. I have a simple bump on my head which will go away."

The swelling went down, but Mr. McGregor was feverish during the night. He dreamed of the two children. They had climbed up the side of the house and were looking at him through the window. Several times he woke groggily and decided to close the drapes, but he was unable to get out of bed, and he could see them quite clearly, pointing and giggling. The boy told him in a solemn whisper that his head was going to drop off, and they would bury it behind the house in a grove of trees. He scolded them and told them that if they didn't go away he would be forced to call their mother.

In the morning he was feeling better. He lunched on cold milk and graham crackers and spent the day cataloguing the things he would collect to take out to the playhouse. At six he pulled the bell-cord. When Billy answered he said, "Have the car ready at nine. We're going out."

There was a long silence on the other end of the tube. "You sure you're all right?"

"Of course I'm all right."

"But you never go out at night. You haven't been out of this house after dinner in over a year."

"You just be ready with the car."

Shortly after nine Billy Easter backed the Lincoln down the driveway and stopped at the gate. It was a warm clear night, perfectly still, with the dark rustle of traffic far below on Sunset Boulevard. Mr. McGregor sat in the rear, bundled up in a heavy topcoat and sweating slightly.

"You wanna give me the key so I can open the gate?" Billy said.

Reluctantly, the old man removed the shoestring from around his neck and handed it over. He hated parting with the key, even for a few seconds. Billy unlocked the gate, creaked it wide open, and drove through. Then he shut it again and returned to the car. "Where to?" he asked.

"The key. May I have it, please?"

The chauffeur flipped it to him. "Don't trust *nobody,*" he muttered.

Mr. McGregor ignored him. "Go to the factory," he said.

"Factory?" Billy turned around in his seat. "It's Sunday night, after nine. Who's gonna be there at this hour?"

"No one. That's why we're going."

Frowning, Billy shifted into gear and the car rolled down the hill. Mr. McGregor studied his dark reflection in the window as they turned onto Sunset Boulevard. The man in the glass had put on a topcoat too, just to mock him.

They veered left into a wide suburban street lined with great trees that reminded him of Michigan in the brittle autumn and of childhood forays into apple orchards. Loretta had never known the change of seasons and neither had his grandchildren. Theirs had been a tropical life, royal palms and pools, sunshine and bathing suits on Christmas morning. If only he had told them about the real sledding winters that crystallized ice on the lips and blew an incredible clarity into the sky.

Soon they were cruising down Santa Monica Boulevard, a dark thoroughfare, badly lit, smelling of the day's smog and the sea. A banjo club was open and college students stood in its entrance, clapping their hands and singing with false enthusiasm. The ocean smell grew stronger, pungent. They had passed the Santa Monica Auditorium, a gigantic building with parking lots like football fields. Mr. McGregor stuffed his restless hands in his pockets. "Don't park too close," he said.

Billy guided the car along a seedy row of lower-class homes and stunted palm trees. MCGREGOR BATHING SUITS was at the far end of the block. He parked a good hundred yards away from the factory. "How's this?" he asked.

"Turn off the lights."

Billy shook his head. "I don't get it. Norman's not here now. There's not a light in the whole place."

"Stay here. I won't be more than ten or fifteen minutes."

Billy grinned into the rearview mirror. "Hey, Mr. McGregor," he said, "you ain't planning on robbing it, are you?"

His hands thrust deep in the pockets of his coat, the old man left the car and walked quickly toward the dark entrance of the building. Hyacinth flooded the night—from where he didn't know. He reached the front door and lingered, scanning the street. No cars, no people. Billy still had his dims on. He signalled but there was no response. Probably fell asleep, he thought. He could drop off like a cat.

He took a pencil flashlight from his pocket and a key. It would still work unless Norman had changed the lock. Checking the street again, he fitted the key in the door and slowly turned it. Then he hesitated, a coldness moving from his hand to his heart. Would Norman have installed an alarm system? The entire city had been wired in the past few years, or so it seemed. Private security services patrolled the sub-urbs. Ferocious dogs prowled department stores at night, trained, he had read, to kill.

Mr. McGregor pushed the door open and waited, breath-ing in a stale waft of weekend air. No sounds assaulted his ears, no alarm bells or sirens. Norman believed in economy; to wire the building, with all the entrances and exits, would have cost thousands. Relieved, Mr. McGregor stepped inside.

Skylights and windows let in a crosscurrent of moonlight that lay like thin silver leaf over the desks. There was a switch by the door that controlled the fluorescent lamps, but he lit his flashlight instead and moved past the receptionist's desk toward the main office area. He heard a fly buzzing; maybe it was his friend from the house, joining him to explore the closed building.

He looked over the long rows of desks. The old furniture was gone; now everything was olive-colored steel, new and alien like samples in a showroom. He preferred the factory as it once was, a big, loft-like structure with secondhand furniture and fans cutting through the cigar smoke. He could see himself then, vital and sharp-tongued, moving around the desks, giving orders, taking phone calls from New York. Where had all that energy gone? Why had his mind wandered to the point where he had forgotten pattern numbers and even, once, the address of the plant? Was it old age, or had the accident permanently dazed him?

Deliberating, Mr. McGregor moved along the lanes of desks, patting work trays full of memos and invoices. There was an answer here, somewhere under the new paint and the new atmosphere. He paused, remembering his mission. Where was the personnel section now after all these years? Mrs. Meltzer used to handle it, a cranky old woman who ate tomato sandwiches for lunch. She had left a month or two before his retirement. But where was her desk, the crucial filing cabinets?

Somewhere, deep in the basement, a door slammed. The old man stiffened, his eyes turning back toward the reception area. He heard the slow drag of footsteps on wooden stairs. There was nowhere to hide in the room.

The footsteps stopped. Someone was standing behind the green-tinted glass partition that divided the executive and working sections. "Who's there?" a voice called. "I can see you."

Mr. McGregor was speechless. He looked for an exit, but the only way out was through the front door, and that was blocked. A flashlight sprang on, a glowing green spray that rippled along the partition. Footsteps made soft, spongy sounds in the deep carpet of the reception area.

Instinctively, Mr. McGregor backed up, almost upsetting a chair. He thought wildly of hiding behind one of the desks, but they were all so small, so skeletal.

"Stay where you are!" A voice commanded. The flashlight beam was suddenly trained on him, hurling his shapeless shadow across the rows of desks. "Mr. McGregor! What are *you* doing here?"

The beam was instantly lowered, and the old man rubbed his eyes. When he opened them he saw little red and yellow worms of light shimmering on the floor. He squinted as the man approached him. It was Fred Schalkenbach, wearing a visored cap and a dark blue uniform that reminded him of a theatre usher.

"Hello, Schalkenbach," Mr. McGregor said uneasily.

Now that he had identified the prowler, Schalkenbach relaxed and grinned. "You're the last person in the world I expected to find in here," he said. "How'd you get in?"

"Key." He held it up, feeling extremely foolish. Here he was, caught in his own building.

"I thought it was some of them teenagers. Figured they must've broken a window or something."

"No." said Mr. McGregor. "Just me."

"What are you doing, looking around?"

"Yes."

Schalkenbach seemed to find this amusing. He took off his coat and hung it over the back of a chair. "Should've tried it during the day. You gave me the fright of my life poking around in here."

"I'm sorry. I guess I should have turned on the lights."

"Checking on your son-in-law? That what you're up to?"

"In a way. I wouldn't mention it if I were you. He might be annoyed."

Schalkenbach laughed; there were gaps in his lower set of dentures. He seemed somewhat unsteady on his feet, like a skater adjusting to solid earth. "I won't say anything," he said. "I think we're old enough friends to keep a secret or two." He removed his hat and placed it on a typewriter. "Damn uniform," he complained. "Makes me feel like I oughta be selling peanuts at a ball game."

Mr. McGregor smiled and remained silent.

"That your car out there? Seems to me I saw a car with its dims on."

"My chauffeur." Mr. McGregor's eyes scanned the desktops. Where was the personnel department?

"That must be nice, having someone drive you around. We'll have to go out sometime, you and me and your chauffeur." He chuckled. "I'd really get a kick outta that."

"Yes." He picked up some papers and riffled through them as if he had business to conduct.

"I know some pretty good bars in Venice. We could have a high old time."

"I shouldn't be disturbing you," Mr. McGregor said. "Don't you have rounds to make?"

"Nothing to worry about. Besides, I'm glad to have you. I go nuts all by myself here at night." He bent over his coat on the chair. "You and me are one up on Norman," he said. "Here's another secret. I got a bottle."

Mr. McGregor opened one of the drawers in the desk. Advertising circulars, layouts.

Schalkenbach dug a pint of liquor from his coat. "Rye," he said. "Good stuff."

Mr. McGregor tried another desk, flipping through the papers on the blotter. More advertising junk—WEAR THE

BEST, WEAR MCGREGOR. He knew they had to maintain personnel files; there was a state law. But what if everything was computerized, stored in the innards of a machine? He'd never be able to get what he wanted.

"Tell you what," said the watchman. "Why don't I dig up some glasses, and we can have ourselves a little night-cap?"

"I don't drink." Mr. McGregor made his voice unfriendly. He wanted the old man to leave him alone.

"Everybody drinks. Puts color in your cheeks. I was going to tell you yesterday at the picnic. You don't look so good. In the old days you were always tan and healthy."

"Go away. Please." Mr. McGregor fumbled open a filing cabinet drawer. "I have work to do."

"Come on," the other man cajoled, opening the bottle. "Don't you remember that time we had the fire? Must've finished a pint, you and me."

Mr. McGregor turned from the filing cabinet and gave him a withering glance. "You heard what I said, Schalkenbach. Go away."

The watchman had the bottle halfway to his lips. He hesitated, baffled by the sudden harshness in the old man's voice. "Just wanted to talk."

"We've talked enough. Now attend to your duties, or I'll be forced to report this incident to Norman."

There was a pause, then Schalkenbach gathered up his coat and hat. "Sorry," he muttered.

Mr. McGregor hated himself for a moment. "Look," he said awkwardly, "I didn't mean—"

But the watchman didn't answer. He had already reached the end of the room and was rounding the glass partition. A few moments later his footfalls sounded on the basement stairs.

Mr. McGregor felt guilty. He should have been more diplomatic. Tomorrow night he would call Schalkenbach and apologize. For some reason he felt a strange kinship with the old man.

The filing cabinets contained the personnel records, three drawers of them on neat blue cards. Half spilling them in his haste he plowed through the 'H's. Hubbard, Hubbard. There—Dorothy Hubbard.

He removed the card from the stack, leaving a gap for its reinsertion, and found a pencil and memo pad on one of the desks. Quickly, he copied the information. *Dorothy Hubbard. Age twenty-eight. Born Salt Lake City. Divorced. Two children: Tod, born 1974, Amy, born 1978. Father, Steven Hubbard, whereabouts unknown. In case of emergency, contact Mrs. Verna Gilchrist (mother) 1617 Adams St., Salt Lake City.* Someone had written in ink above the mother's name: "Now deceased."

The address—where the devil was the address? He turned over the card and found it written in pencil on the back: *10458 Alameda, West Los Angeles.* It was only a few miles from the factory.

Mr. McGregor felt a momentary surge of elation. They were near, close by. It was almost as if he could reach out and touch them. He pocketed the information, returned the card to the files, and quickly moved toward the door, thinking about the birth dates of the children. The boy Tod would be ten, and the girl was six. Mark had been nine when he died; Ruthie had been six.

Billy Easter's head was pressed against the steering wheel. He was dozing. Mr. McGregor shook him awake. "I'm finished. Set your alarm for seven-thirty tomorrow morning."

"Seven-thirty?"

"On the button." Mr. McGregor settled himself comfortably in the back seat. "The early bird catches the worm."

As the car pulled away from the curb he looked back at the dark building. A dim face was pressed to the glass of the front door. I'll call you, Schalkenbach, he promised. Sooner or later we'll have that drink together.

Billy Easter couldn't figure it out. Here it was eight-fifteen in the morning, and they were parked miles from the estate on a tiny street lined with ramshackle houses and garden court apartments. And there was crazy old McGregor, bright as a bird, sitting in the rear with a big black cigar. He was up to something, sure as rain, and Billy Easter didn't like the smell of it. "Who we waiting for?" he asked.

"No one in particular, Billy. It's a business matter. You should have brought your paper."

Making sure the old man couldn't see, Billy opened the flap of his tunic pocket and felt inside. He touched his bone, the new one that had just arrived from the store in downtown Los Angeles. It was larger than the last, infinitely more powerful—or at least that's what his friends had claimed. This one he'd carry wherever he went. He'd never again make the mistake of leaving it exposed over the door of his room. That was begging for trouble with a crazy old man loose in the house, and he had learned his lesson the hard way.

The smoke from the cigar lapped around his face, and he had the panicky feeling that they were going to sit there all morning while McGregor spewed out his smoke like a volcano, calm, patient, and secretly pleased with himself.

Billy sneaked a view of the old man in his mirror. He was studying one of the houses across the street, a sagging bungalow with a wide porch and adjustable awnings that could be raised and lowered in a city where it hardly ever rained. A bike was sprawled on the front steps. "Can't we get some breakfast," Billy said.

"Later."

It was a dead morning on a dead street, and Billy was already bored. He watched as a Mexican gardener turned a water faucet on the side of an old apartment house. Blue jets of water gushed from hidden sprinklers along the pavement and soon a fine, rainbow mist was blowing toward them. He would have liked to be out there in his bathing trunks, darting through the spray, drinking cold water right from the faucet.

Mr. McGregor suddenly muttered something to himself as two children came out of the bungalow and leapt over the stranded bike. The boy wore a blue blazer with a matching cap; the girl wore the same kind of coat and cap and a blue plaid skirt.

"Start the motor," the old man said tensely.

Billy twisted the ignition key. Now what was all this? Up at seven in the morning to follow two school kids? He felt inside his pocket again and rubbed the bone.

They cruised slowly down the block. The children abruptly ducked into an empty lot, kicking at cans and loose stones as they ran.

"Don't lose them," said Mr. McGregor. He was leaning on the window, his head thrust out like an old dog sniffing the wind.

Disgusted, Billy swung the car along another street that paralleled the vacant lot. Chasing kids when he could be home asleep.

A school bus was parked on the intersecting street, its motor idling while the driver supervised a group of youngsters clambering aboard. A large red seal on its side read: FRIENDS OF THE SACRED HEART ACADEMY.

The old man leaned forward and drummed on Billy's back. "Stop right here," he whispered. More thick fumes from the cigar. Billy braked with a lurch, tossing the old man against the cushions. He laughed soundlessly to himself.

47

Across the street the children churned around the bus, most of them wearing blue coats and caps. There was something funny and likable about them to Billy Easter. He enjoyed the way they grabbed at each other's school books and took long giant steps into the bus. The driver was frazzled; he banged on the side windows and shouted for the ones inside to settle down. When they were all loaded, including Mr. McGregor's two little friends, the driver got in and closed the door.

"I guess we follow them," said Billy.

"That's correct."

They rumbled through the hazy deserted streets, the school bus crawling at a safe thirty miles an hour. Some of the children were huddled at the rear window, drawing with their fingers on the glass. One of them suddenly pointed.

"They see us," said Mr. McGregor. "Slow down. Get behind that other car."

Billy obeyed grudgingly. He yearned for his pillow and a secret morning sip of rum. Thinking of liquor reminded him that he was desperately hungry. "When are we going to eat?" he asked.

"Later. Just keep your eyes on that bus."

They were now on a clean, well-shaded boulevard that ran along the edge of Brentwood. Billy was sure that movie stars lived nearby in the hundreds. He allowed two cars to fill the gap in front of him, but one of them turned off without signalling and the bus loomed up again with its string of faces at the window.

"Slower," Mr. McGregor said, jabbing him in the back.

There was a red light, and he pumped the brakes, angling into the far lane so that a Mercedes could move up behind the bus. The light blinked, and the bus started up slowly, its old gears shifting and creaking. Billy hung back, remaining in the new lane, while the Mercedes honked its horn impatiently and finally shot ahead. Go, buddy, go,

Billy Easter sang to himself. He watched, impressed, as it streaked down the boulevard, all speed and power.

The game continued for another few miles, and Billy began to enjoy it. He cut in and out of traffic while great royal palms swept past like feather dusters, and the sun burned through the smog.

The bus signalled with a little metal flap that clapped against its side like a hand. It took a right turn up a short incline, and Billy reduced his speed. The red seal on the bus was duplicated on a sign that hung over the pebbled drive: FRIENDS OF THE SACRED HEART ACADEMY. A plaster angel leaned out from the bordering trees, its chipped arms raised protectively. "What kind of place is this?" he asked.

"Parochial school."

"Christian place?"

"Mmmm."

The bus had stopped in a gravel parking area. Women in dark robes were waiting at the gate, and as the children poured from the bus the sisters fluttered about like blackbirds. Behind the gate was a large building, Spanish and low, honeycombed with inner courtyards where men were hosing down the dusty tile. Another angel, white and glazed like a wedding cake, crouched near a tall bell tower. Its face was sunny and fatherly. The children, guided by the women, had formed a long, bobbing blue line and were half-running, half-walking toward the entrance of the building.

"You going to school?" Billy Easter asked. "Or, do we hustle up some breakfast?"

Mr. McGregor waited until one of the nuns closed the heavy wooden door. The bell tolled twice, frightening birds that rustled up from the lawn. "Go back to Alameda," he said. The burnt-down cigar looked like a charred cork in his mouth. "There's something I have to check."

"We were just there."

"Don't worry about it. We'll pick you up a newspaper on the way."

Billy drove slowly past the ramshackle bungalow on Alameda, his stomach making noises. Mr. McGregor was poking him in the back again. "Look at the garage in the rear," the old man said. "Is that a car?"

"Sure is. You better buy yourself some glasses."

"Park on the other side of the street."

Billy stopped at the curb and turned off the ignition. A new cigar was going in the back seat. He decided they'd probably sit there all day without food or even a chance to stretch their stiff legs. The neighborhood had changed by now: women were hanging wash in the yards, and people were sitting around the pool at the corner apartment house. He picked up the newspaper.

"Look!" said Mr. McGregor, pointing at the bungalow.

Billy turned to see what the old man had discovered. Someone was pulling the drapes aside, opening the window to let in air.

"Can you make out who it is?"

"Woman," Billy said, straining his eyes. "Wearing a bathrobe."

Bright blonde hair caught the sunlight, then the window was empty. The old man watched for a few more minutes, his face puzzled.

Billy flung the newspaper aside. Now what was going on here? That crazy old man couldn't be interested in a young blonde. The thought was so improbable that he almost broke out laughing. Maybe the devils bottled up inside him wanted some action, felt like kicking up their heels. "Who's that lady?" he asked.

"Never mind. Just find me a drugstore. I need a telephone."

Billy drove off, his mind boiling with possibilities. If McGregor was really after the blonde there might be fun for all concerned. Providing, of course, that she wanted to play along. But what the hell did the kids have to do with it? Unless the old man was smarter than he looked, unless he was waiting till the kids were at school, and he had a clear field. Maybe that was it.

There was a drugstore on the corner, and Billy found a vacant parking space. "Stay in the car," the old man instructed him. "I won't be long."

As soon as he had gone inside, Billy climbed out and crossed to the drugstore window. The sun glared on the glass, but he could see the old man heading for a bank of phone booths in the rear. He lingered at the window for a moment and then entered the store, whistling cockily as if he owned the place.

Passing the magazine stand, he edged up to the booth and glanced around to see if anyone was watching. There was only a clerk, stacking toothpaste cartons on the dental display. He leaned toward the door of the booth, listening.

". . . Mrs. Hubbard there?" the old man was saying. His voice sounded different, deeper. "Oh? She's not at work today. . . . I see. Well, I guess if she's feeling better she'll be in tomorrow. . . . Nothing important. I'll call back then."

Billy barely had time to turn toward the magazine stand before the door snapped open, and Mr. McGregor plunged out, wiping his flushed face with a handkerchief. But he wasn't quick enough—the old man saw him. "I thought I told you to stay in the car."

"Can't I get a magazine? I got tired of that newspaper."

"You were eavesdropping." Mr. McGregor's eyes narrowed, bunching up like caterpillars.

"No I wasn't. I just wanted something to read."

The old man grabbed a magazine. "Go back to the car. I'll pay for this."

Billy hurried from the store. Something was cooking, all right, something shady. The old man was checking on the blonde, using a disguised voice on the phone. He could keep his reasons secret for a while, but sooner or later he'd need Billy to help him. And that's when it would start costing him money.

Whistling brokenly through his teeth, Billy slid behind the wheel of the car. He tapped his hands on the dashboard in time with the rhythm. Straw hats, ladies' handbags. Eighty-six proof rum, no duty. He could see his tin hut shimmering in the Jamaican sun, the rich white palms of tourists. All he had to do was wait.

The house on Alameda was closed and silent, the bike casting a blue shadow on the steps. The front window was still open, and its drapes hung motionless in the noon heat. Billy had finished reading the magazine and had propped it over his head like a paper tent. Mr. McGregor sat in the back seat, his face pressed to the window, working on his third cigar.

"Eat," Billy said. "When are we going to eat?"

"Later. I'll buy you a steak."

Billy looked under the flap of paper at the house. Someone was jiggling the front door from the inside. An instant later it opened, and the blonde came out, closing it carefully behind her. Billy's lips framed a silent whistle. The old man might be coasting downhill in his sixties but he could still pick 'em. That little girl had on stretch pants and a tight jersey that showed just about all she had without much fuss. Her feet were tucked into gold sandals that flashed like mirrors when she walked. The Mexican gardener across the street laid down his shears and stood up to get a better view. "Call the fire department," Billy Easter laughed. "Somebody put a hose on that blaze."

"Quiet," Mr. McGregor ordered. He hadn't moved a muscle.

The girl went around the side of the house, and then an old Buick convertible backed down the drive into the street. It was painted emerald green and a taillight was broken. The girl was driving, a thin rose scarf over her hair.

"*This* one I'll follow," said Billy Easter, throwing the car in gear.

"Don't get too close," said Mr. McGregor. "But don't lose her either."

"I ain't planning to."

The girl drove in the direction of Beverly Hills. Billy was disappointed; he had hoped she was going to the beach where he might have seen her in a bathing suit. But he followed her as she swept down Wilshire Boulevard, increasing her speed. As they continued to drive away from the ocean it grew brighter and hotter; he felt the intake vents pouring baking air on his knees. The Hollywood Hills, off to the left, were half hidden by haze.

The Buick stopped at a light, and Billy inched up two cars behind. He noticed that a little girl's doll was stuck up over the back seat of the convertible. "Those were her kids, huh?" he said, surprised that a woman so youthful had children.

"Concentrate on your driving," Mr. McGregor muttered.

Billy hummed a light, skipping tune. Straw hats and ladies' handbags. The old man was really looking for trouble. He couldn't pick a woman closer to his own age; he had to go searching for one with kids.

A block past La Cienega, the Buick cut its speed and slipped into a space in front of a small bar. Billy shot by looking for a parking spot. It was early afternoon, and most of the spaces were taken.

"Let me out," the old man said, reaching for the door. "You can drive around and pick me up later."

"Have a heart," said Billy. "Can't I get a ginger ale in that bar? My throat's so dry, I can hardly swallow."

The car stopped, and Mr. McGregor stumbled over the curb, half-tripping. "All right," he called back. "Ginger ale but no beer."

"Cross my heart." He floored the accelerator and shot up a side street. He'd stick to ginger ale all right. Clear head, clear eyes. There were things brewing, and he didn't want to miss any of them.

Mr. McGregor felt conspicuous in his dark blue suit and conservative tie. The men at the bar were dressed in sports clothes, and he could feel their eyes assessing him in the mirror. The Hubbard woman was sitting in a booth by herself, looking down morosely at the table.

Removing his coat and loosening his tie, he wedged himself up to the bar and ordered a beer. He paid for it and took a few cool, refreshing sips while he inspected the room. It had the cloistered look of similar establishments in the early afternoon. Outside the hot sun was shining, but in here was the smell and gloom of the pre-dawn hours. He wondered what the mother of two young children was doing in such a place. And why had she called in sick to the office?

Casually, not wishing to direct attention to himself, he took his glass to the rear. There was an empty booth behind the Hubbard woman, and he occupied it.

The bartender strolled up to her. "How goes it?" he asked.

"So-so, Leo. I could use one of your daiquiris."

"Jay called, said to tell you he'd be late."

"That bastard," the woman said evenly.

The bartender laughed. "Two of my daiquiris, and you'll forget him."

"Two of your daiquiris, and you and me'll get married."

Mr. McGregor sat perfectly still while the bartender went back to the counter. The woman seemed agitated; her nails tapped on the wooden table. He could hear a match scratching into flame.

The door to the street opened, a square of white blinding light, and Billy Easter came in sheepishly. He glanced in the old man's direction and then crossed to the bar. Mr. McGregor hoped he wouldn't join him.

The bartender returned with the drink. "Don't see much of Jay anymore," he said. "Hear he's up for a picture."

"He's always up for a picture. Cheers. If I had a nickel for every picture he didn't make, I'd have me a house in Malibu."

"All he needs is some luck."

"Don't we all."

Cynical, Mr. McGregor thought. Why is a young girl like that so cynical?

The door opened again and a young man came in; Mr. McGregor could see him clearly. He was no more than thirty, a powerfully built man with shaggy sideburns and a light-blond mustache. He slid into the Hubbard woman's booth and said, "Hi, honey." There were soft nuzzling sounds, punctuated by the man's dry cough. "Gotta get more sleep," he said. "This kinda life's gonna put me in a TB ward."

"When are you going to break down and buy a wristwatch?" the woman asked.

He laughed. "Thought you'd give me one for my birthday. What are you drinking?"

"Daiquiri. It's very bad for guys who don't get enough sleep."

"Think I'll have one on you," he said. Mr. McGregor could hear more soft, nuzzling sounds. "You look sort of puffy yourself, honey."

"Amy woke up in the middle of the night with a stomachache. I was crawling in closets at three in the morning looking for milk of magnesia."

"Poor, poor Dot," the man said in a lilting, singsong voice. "Had her fun and now she hates wiping its nose."

"*Two* noses."

They both laughed. The bartender brought drinks over to the table. "Everybody's happy," he said. "That's what I like to see."

"Congratulate us, Leo," the man said.

"What for?"

"Dorothy and me are thinking of getting married."

"Well!" said the bartender. "I didn't know."

The girl interrupted, her voice hoarse with smoke. "Don't believe him. Jay's been dancing around that particular subject for almost a year. Ask him to show you the ring."

"So where is it?" Leo asked, laughing. To Mr. McGregor's delicate ear he sounded slightly embarrassed.

"Who has money for a ring?" Jay said. "I'll pick one up in a Cracker Jack box."

"Invite me to the wedding," said Leo. "See you later. I've got customers."

The bartender's face dipped over Mr. McGregor's table. "You want a refill, Pop?"

"I'm fine."

The couple in the next booth waited until they were alone again. "What's this marriage talk?" said Dorothy.

"Why not? Maybe it's time. And you can't get enough of me, can you, lover?"

"Don't count on it."

"The kids are a problem, though." Jay's voice was

thoughtful. "But we can figure something out. I might be coming into some money."

"Sure. Put it on a record and play it at night."

"Marty seems pretty high on this picture. Eight weeks in Puerto Rico, all expenses paid."

"Agent talk," Dorothy said. "Who's making this little gem, Bankrupt Productions?"

"Dunno. Marty says they've got money."

"Marry Marty," she said. "At least he believes in your future."

Mr. McGregor gripped the edge of his table. He despised both of them, the girl more than the man. She was so dreadfully coarse, a creature of impulse and appetite; there was nothing even remotely maternal about her. She had no right to the children, no right at all.

"I'll be leaving next week if it goes through. We could get married over the weekend."

The girl was silent. Mr. McGregor could hear her lighting another cigarette. "You really gang up on me," she said finally. "All I wanted was a few drinks. Now it's suddenly problem time."

"No problem, lover," Jay said softly. "You know what you want to do. Go with your instincts. Meet me in Puerto Rico and we'll make a honeymoon out of it."

"Turn it off," she said. "It's not going to happen."

Jay stood up. "Come on back to the place. I've got a new air conditioner."

"Your car's in hock but you buy an air conditioner. I've got a nine-year-old son who can think circles around you."

"Come on," he said gently, guiding her out of the booth. "There's a half-bottle of brandy left over from Saturday."

The girl glanced unseeingly at Mr. McGregor. "Puerto Rico and brandy. I come pretty high, don't I?"

Jay laughed and took her hand. Mr. McGregor watched

them as they went toward the door. The man's hair rippled over his collar, and the girl massaged the small of his back with possessive, circular movements. Billy Easter gave them a searching look as they went out.

The old man remained at his table, thinking of the two children running toward school while the sisters swooped protectively around them. He remembered the little girl holding out her arm to show him the cut. He rose from the booth and looked down at the next table where a lipsticked cigarette, still burning, was sending up a column of smoke.

Out on the glaring street he walked a few blind yards, his head pounding with the old headache. Billy came tagging after him, wiping beer foam from his mouth. "Where to now?" he asked eagerly.

"Anywhere at all," Mr. McGregor said.

As they drove up the long hill to the estate he felt better. He always loved the wild oak that grew in blurred circles around his house. It was still home, a place to hide, even though it no longer contained his daughter's presence and the voices of children. Night was coming; there was already a hush under the heat, a blue shadow like a frown on the brow of the hill. They had exhausted the afternoon by driving aimlessly along the ocean while Mr. McGregor sorted his thoughts and decided what he had to do.

Nearing the house, he was surprised to see Norman's car parked in the driveway. It was a new Jaguar, its roof liquid with the reflection of trees. But Norman wasn't in it. The old man was alarmed—how had he gotten through the gates? Then he realized that his son-in-law must still have a key from the old days. It seemed that everyone had keys to everything.

Billy parked at the front door of the house, but the old man sat brooding. Norman hadn't paid a visit in ages, not since Loretta had been put away. He didn't like the idea of him poking around the estate when no one was home.

As he climbed out of the car, Norman came around the side of the house and waved to him. He was wearing a burnt-orange corduroy suit and a green hat with a feather in the band. "What's that boat doing in the backyard?" he asked.

Mr. McGregor felt as if he had been abruptly backed into a corner. "I—had it built," he said lamely.

Norman frowned at him. "Why?"

"It's for Mark."

"Mark?" His son-in-law seemed confused. "I don't get it."

"Really, it's quite simple. A long time ago he told me he wanted a playhouse inside a boat—he even used to draw pictures of it. I—well, I suppose I wanted to make his wish come true."

Norman nodded, but an odd, removed expression came over his face. "That's a nice thought," he said. "I'm sure Mark would have appreciated it. But couldn't you have just put flowers on the grave or something?"

"It wouldn't have been the same at all," Mr. McGregor said. "I'm going to put all their old toys in there."

Norman shrugged. "If that's what you want. . . ." There was obviously something else on his mind, something disturbing. "Dad, the reason I came up here—what were you doing in the plant last night?"

Mr. McGregor tried to conceal his surprise. He glanced away and saw that Billy was pretending to polish the side mirror of the car. "I suppose Schalkenbach told you," he said.

"Came to me first thing this morning. Said you were going through the files."

"He should mind his own business." The old man was annoyed at himself for not having shared a drink with the night watchman. "It's still my plant, Norman."

"Dad," said Norman patiently, "you had every right to be there. But at night, with a flashlight?"

"I didn't want to disturb you. I know how busy you are during the day."

Norman sighed. "Suppose Schalkenbach had called the police? Did you ever think of that?"

Mr. McGregor pinched the bridge of his nose, stalling for time. Apologies and excuses multiplied in his mind, but none of them seemed appropriate. "I'm awfully tired, Norman. Can't we discuss this tomorrow?"

"But what were you doing there on a Sunday night?"

"Nothing in particular. Just looking around."

"You should have come in during the day. I'm never busy for you, am I?"

"I wanted to see it after dark," the old man explained. "When I was just starting out, I used to work in the evenings. It was quiet and relaxing. No one was around to bother me. Do you know what I mean?"

Something had softened in Norman's eyes. "Yeah," he acknowledged reflectively. "Almost seems as if I can get twice as much work done at night. But Sharon doesn't like me keeping late hours."

"I really wasn't there to work," Mr. McGregor admitted. "I just wanted to see the place again. I'm sorry I disturbed your watchman."

Norman took out his car keys and very carefully spun them between his thumb and forefinger. "Sure you wouldn't like to come back in an advisory capacity?" he asked. "Is that what you're hinting at?"

Mr. McGregor forced a broad smile. "Lord no. I'm too old to be stirring up trouble. I enjoy being retired."

The younger man's eyes, under the green hat, were

guarded. "Suppose I give you a look at the new line?"

"Couldn't be less interested. It's your business now. You've done quite well with it, and I'm proud of you."

Norman seemed pleased with the compliment. "Tell you what," he said. "Why don't we have lunch together next week? There's a great new spot on the beach."

"I'd like that."

"Good. I'll give you a call." He pulled on his neat leather driving gloves, smoothing them down over each finger, and climbed into the car. "If you like boating so much, we could go sailing one of these weekends."

"Just stationary boats," the old man said.

Norman nodded and gave a brisk wave. He wheeled the Jaguar around the front of the house and headed down the drive under the darkening trees. Mr. McGregor watched him go with a feeling of relief. It had been a contest for a few moments, but he had handled it adroitly. And there would certainly be no sailing expeditions or lunches. The old man decided that he would not call his son-in-law for a long time. Perhaps he would even have the phone disconnected.

Billy Easter was still laboriously polishing the side mirror. Mr. McGregor turned on him. "Did you get an earful?" he snapped. "That's as shiny as it's ever going to get. I want dinner in an hour."

Billy hurried into the house, and Mr. McGregor stood looking out over the lawns of his estate. The air was a rich plum color like ice on a Michigan lake. Why had he never taken his grandchildren back to that frozen country in the glorious middle of winter?

He went through the front door into a living room that still smelled of warm afternoon. His favorite chair stood near the fireplace. He dropped into it and laced his fingers across his stomach, giving himself up to plans and speculations.

61

* * *

The Sacred Heart Academy was deserted, its white walls broken by shadow and the dry pollen of moonlight. Mr. McGregor sat huddled in the back seat of the car, watching the school over the red rim of his cigar. Across the patio a light was burning. It looked tiny and fragile like a small cluster of candles. "Drive through that other gate," he told Billy Easter. "Let's see where it leads."

The car swung silently past the school and then out through a row of heavy trees to a dark residential street. It was certainly an expensive neighborhood, the old man thought, inspecting the rows of homes on their sharply sloping lawns. One of them, a large colonial house, had a sign attached to a pole in the grass.

"Turn up that drive," Mr. McGregor ordered, "and cut your headlights."

When they reached the front drive of the colonial house, he looked down through the rear window of the car. Across the street was a wall of shrubbery fencing off the school, but the building itself and its adjoining playground were spread out cleanly like a moonlit map. The view was clear enough for him to see the discolorations in the smooth concrete of the yard.

Mr. McGregor got out of the car and walked over to the sign. FOR RENT, FURNISHED it read. And then in smaller, scroll-like letters: *Circle Real Estate. 213 Canon Drive, Beverly Hills*.

The old man jotted down the address on a card in his wallet and then moved cautiously around the house, studying it from all angles. It was separated from its neighbors on three sides by thick gleaming rows of acacia and the little white ladders of rose trellises. The other homes loomed up nearby, but the shrubbery made an excellent natural wall.

Satisfied, Mr. McGregor went back to the car. If he remembered correctly, there was an old black suit layered in moth balls somewhere in the attic. That and a white shirt with an old-fashioned removable collar would be perfect for his impersonation. "Nine o'clock tomorrow," he said to Billy.

Bea Devereaux detested Los Angeles with a grim and sullen fierceness that surprised her. She was new at her job and new in the city, and she hated the dry, dead streets, the terrible sunlight that chased her wherever she went. At times she cried herself to sleep, dreaming she was back in big wet Louisiana with great storm clouds building over the Gulf. She felt as if she were living in a foreign country, and she was even ashamed of her rich accent in a city where the people spoke a neutral, television-announcer English. Even her new job depressed her—guiding couples through overpriced, underbuilt mansions in the heart of Beverly Hills.

There was a gentle knock on her office door. Bea rose quickly, smoothing her new California dress and arranging her facial muscles into the thin imitation of a smile. It was her noon appointment, a priest, and she commanded herself to relax. She was a Roman Catholic, and even though the father was a Los Angelino, at least he was a member of the same faith.

He nodded at her and took a seat in one of her plastic chairs. He seemed a strange man with his weak blue eyes flitting nervously over the room. She didn't like the way his white hair was soaked down with water and the orange sunlight glowed through his enormous ears. The black clerical suit was well-pressed but it seemed dusty, stiff as cardboard. "You said over the phone that you were interested in a particular house, Father?"

"Yes." The old man's watery eyes wouldn't stop wandering. "The colonial on Poinsettia Drive."

Bea smiled. "We just put it up last week."

"I'd like to see it," the priest said. His white fingers fluttered on his trousers. The suit, Bea noticed, smelled vaguely of gardenias.

"Why certainly, Father. Although it might be a bit too large for you. It's three bedrooms, a library, kitchen, maid's room and den."

"It's not just for me. I have two friends of the cloth who will be moving in."

Bea smiled her professional smile. "That would make it perfect," she said. "It's four thousand a month, you know. Would that be too steep?"

"No," the priest said, his hands opening and closing. A fly was buzzing in the corner, and the sound seemed to distract him. "No, that sounds just about right for us."

Bea was privately impressed. Most of the priests she knew were lucky to afford modest homes or apartments near their parishes. Perhaps here in California they were paid a great deal more. "Why don't I drive you out?" she asked. "We can take a tour of the house and grounds. Give you an idea of what you'd be getting."

"I'd appreciate that." The old man's eyes were still on the corner of the room where the fly buzzed.

"Don't know how it got in here," she said absently. "I'll have to get the spray can."

"Don't kill it," the priest said sharply. "Just open the window. It'll fly out."

Bea flushed. Couldn't she do anything right? Priests were preservers of life. There was a father once in a little plaster Gulf Coast parish who refused to kill a water moccasin that had crawled into the rectory through the floorboards. They had waited until he left for dinner before three men crushed it with sticks. "I'll leave the window open while we're gone," she said.

He nodded somberly and followed her out into the terrifying sunlight.

She enjoyed showing the old priest through the empty house. It was a typical "delta colonial," wide and soundly constructed, a harbor against hurricanes. It reminded her of her grandfather's home in Shreveport with its high rooms and monstrous closets. She almost felt like moving in herself and shutting out the California landscape.

She led the old man through the ground floor and then up the white wooden stairway to the second level. She noticed with surprise that he wasn't listening to a word of her sales pitch. His face was blank, his eyes drifting along the carpet. "And this is the master bedroom," she said, hoping to arouse his interest.

"Hmmm." He might just as easily be standing in a hotel lobby for all the attention he was paying. Then he saw the window that overlooked the street. He crossed to it with a sudden quickness and leaned close to the pane. Bea moved up behind him. Far below, across the street, she could see a school yard where the flying figures of children shimmered behind the trees. The priest was watching the scene with a rapt expression; his hands scratched each other behind his back. She noticed that his fingernails were yellowed, like bits of bone.

"It's a lovely view, isn't it?" she said.

"Yes." He didn't take his eyes from the window.

His terseness began to worry her; she was suddenly afraid that something was wrong. Perhaps he didn't like the house now that he'd had a firsthand look. Maybe he wanted something more contemporary. Panicking, she said, "The owner is a motion picture producer. He and his family are off to Europe, Italy I think. They'd like to sublet for a year."

The old man nodded. He appeared bored, almost apathetic. Bea tried to calm herself, remembering her real estate training. Never oversell a client. "Would you like to see the grounds?" she asked. "They have a beautiful garden."

"It won't be necessary," the priest said.

Bea sighed. Well, she had tried. Her worst fault was her optimism, her belief that other people shared her tastes.

"Everything seems to be in order," the old man said. "I suppose you'd like at least two months' rent in advance."

She stared at him. Did he actually intend to take it? Yet there he was, a dusty old cleric with a hole in his sock, busily counting out one-hundred-dollar bills from a damp wallet. Had he robbed a bank? The thought shocked her, and she managed a wavering smile. "In cash?" she asked.

"Always."

"Well—well I don't have my receipt book with me." She fumbled in her purse, bringing up her sunglasses for no apparent reason.

"Just write it down on the back of one of your calling cards. You can send me the contracts later."

Bea glanced down at the enormous stack of money. It was real. "All right," she said hesitantly. She couldn't quite bring herself to fold the money and put it away. She wasn't even sure there was room for it in her purse. "When do you think you'll be moving in?"

"Tonight, probably."

Bea studied him. He seemed more alive now, more agitated; there was a slight flush on his face. The strands of his coarse old hair were dried, and they stood up at odd angles. He hovered over her shoulder as she made out the receipt on the bedroom cosmetic table. Some of the ink splurted on the card. "Oh, I'm sorry," she cried, dabbing it with a piece of tissue. "I'll give you another one."

"Don't bother. This is fine."

As she led him out to the car, she still felt bewildered. "If you call me, I'll give you a list of the utility people you'll have to contact," she said.

The priest nodded. He seemed pleased now, hoarding his satisfaction like a miser. The blue eyes no longer wandered. Bea could feel their heavy pressure on her face as she guided the car through the traffic on Sunset Boulevard.

When they arrived in Beverly Hills, she dropped him off outside her office. He started to walk away, then he turned and came back to the car. His face bobbed close to hers, the skin pink as a rabbit's. "Don't forget the fly," he said.

"No. No, of course not."

He stood poised for a moment, perplexed, as if he couldn't quite believe that their business was complete. Then he swung away down the street, the sunlight running off his shiny black suit.

The next morning they stopped at a camera and optical shop in Westwood Village. Mr. McGregor paid cash for a powerful pair of field glasses. He had the case wrapped in an anonymous white box so that Billy Easter couldn't see it.

Then they drove to the colonial house. The rental agent had left the key in the mailbox, and the old man placed the envelope in his pocket and instructed Billy to park in the garage.

"We moving out of the other place?" the black man asked.

"No. We'll only be here temporarily."

"Who owns this dump?"

67

"I do."

Billy gave him a sharp, surprised glance. Go ahead, mull that over, the old man thought. Billy was growing too suspicious, too interested in his affairs. He'd have to be paid off soon and released. But for the present he was still valuable.

They entered the house through the garage. Bea had opened all the curtains in the living room, and Mr. McGregor immediately closed them. He went to the kitchen and lowered the blinds over the sink, telling Billy to get the picnic hamper and the magazines from the car.

When Billy returned he was frowning. "We gonna camp out here all day?"

"A few hours. Maybe less."

Sulkily, Billy sat down on a kitchen chair and cupped his hands under his chin. He flipped through one of the magazines without reading it.

The refrigerator was humming in the corner. Mr. McGregor unpacked the hamper, transferring a thermos jug and wax-papered sandwiches onto the gleaming wire shelves. "If you get hungry, there's plenty of food in the icebox."

Billy's shoulders lifted in acknowledgment, then dropped. "You going out?"

"I'll be upstairs. I don't want to be disturbed."

"Suppose I run out of magazines?"

"You won't."

Mr. McGregor closed the kitchen door, walked down the hallway, and climbed to the second floor. The bedroom blazed with sunlight; great golden shafts poured on a huge Navajo rug that lapped at the edge of his feet like a pool. He shut the door and edged close to the window. Far below the Sacred Heart Academy shimmered in the heat, a block of vanilla ice cream. It was shortly after noon, and the building seemed to be drowsing; the only movement was a gardener dragging a long coil of hose. The empty playground baked in the sun. The heat waves rising from the concrete seemed blue and gaseous, and the whole yard trembled gently like a mirage.

Mr. McGregor unwrapped the binoculars and pulled a chair across the floor to the window. It would probably be a long wait, and he hoped Billy wouldn't grow restless. He scanned the street. As far as he could tell, no one had seen them arrive. The car was safely in the garage, and the house, with its curtained windows, still gave the appearance of being empty.

He brought the heavy pair of binoculars to his eyes. The sun would probably flash on the lenses, warning anyone on the school grounds who happened to look up. But at a distance it could be the light striking a window or glancing off an aluminum blind.

The scene was blurred through the lenses. Mr. McGregor fiddled impatiently with the sighting rings, his arms propped on the windowsill. Then the confusion cleared, and the school jumped up mirror-bright. The building was much closer now; he could even make out the rough texture of the stone.

Amazing. Truly amazing. The old man smiled under his new iron spectacles. He shifted his arms on the sill and found himself looking at the leaves on the trees. With two or three times the optical power it might be possible to see insects crawling along, feeding on the waxy surfaces.

There was a sudden wave of voices, tumbling down and spilling into the air. Mr. McGregor tilted the binoculars and saw a flood of children pouring from the rear of the school. They were surging across the playground toward a jungle gym that stood in the center of the yard. Some veered off, spinning and pushing each other, but most went plunging toward the top.

Mr. McGregor closed his eyes tightly. He felt sick. He knew what would happen if he continued to watch. Perhaps if he didn't look he could cheat the accident. Sweating, he lowered the binoculars a fraction and trained them on a group playing jacks. The sun seemed to be directly overhead, and there were no shadows anywhere. The entire yard was alive with children, a shifting tangle of heads and dresses and skinned knees. Occasionally one of the sisters would emerge from the welter, her cowled head peeking over the children like a tulip.

Desperately, Mr. McGregor moved the binoculars across the field of view, searching for the two familiar faces. He knew it was an impossible task—there were too many bodies in the yard, all of them moving too fast. Once he thought he saw Amy at the drinking fountain, but when the little girl turned he realized it was someone else. There was no sign of Tod. The boys in the crowd seemed older; they probably came from a higher grade.

The chapel bell rang and the group was herded into parallel lines to be led back into the building. A few stragglers were rounded up by the patrolling nuns and once again the yard was empty. The old man sat back in the chair, wiping his sweating forehead. The binoculars had pressed two indentations around the rims of his eyes, and he massaged the tender skin.

He sat perfectly still for a long time in the hot light from the window, desiring his own cool room where he could stretch out on the bed while the afternoon ran down. But there was no time for rest, he had to remain alert. The school had its routine. It would probably require days, even weeks, before he could work out a timetable.

Voices again, rising from the yard. The old man grabbed the binoculars and brought them up to his eyes. Another group had come clamoring from the building, this one composed of boys closer to Tod's age. Again most were drawn to the jungle gym where they climbed and clustered like flies.

Mr. McGregor carefully studied their faces. There were fewer this time, and he moved the glasses slowly from one corner of the yard to another, covering every square inch of the playground. He passed over a trio that was squatting on the concrete and then, on a second thought, he shifted back to them. Yes! There was Tod, sitting on his blue school jacket, playing some kind of game with paper squares. Even from the great distance the old man could recognize the dark little boy's tense posture and brooding eyes. His hair seemed flat and shiny, as if it were wetted down with tonic.

Mr. McGregor concentrated on the trio, his arms balanced on the sill. He wasn't prepared when Tod suddenly darted away from the others, leaving his section of the frame empty. Grumbling to himself, the old man inched the binoculars in the direction of the boy's flight and finally picked him up near the edge of the playground. Tod glanced over his shoulder once or twice, then vanished.

Mr. McGregor blinked rapidly, unable to believe his eyes. The boy was gone; it was almost as if the concrete was water, and he had sunk without a bubble. But that was impossible. Perhaps he had returned to the game with the paper squares. The old man frantically swung the glasses back to the other boys, but Tod hadn't rejoined them.

Over the other faces again. Slowly, very slowly. He must be somewhere, hiding behind the drinking fountain, shielded by a sister's black skirts. But he was not in the yard, and the old man felt a certain loneliness, as if the sun had clouded over, and he was watching a playground full of shadows.

The bell rang, three swollen notes summoning the children back to their classes. The nuns were swooping again, gathering up their flock into manageable lines. The old man ran the binoculars down each column, his eyes straining, but the boy wasn't among them. The lines marched into the building and the playground was suddenly empty. The little paper squares lay on the ground, weighed down by the heat. The yard shimmered.

Sadly, the old man lowered the binoculars. Maybe the boy never really existed; the two children at the picnic had been products of his imagination. Then he caught a flash from below. There was Tod, racing along the playground toward the building, his jacket flapping behind him like a flag. He had appeared from nowhere, moving in long bounds across the concrete. He reached the rear door of the school and slipped inside.

Mr. McGregor couldn't understand it. He was bringing up the binoculars again when he heard a sound behind him. He turned in the chair, listening. There was the soft tremor of someone breathing. Clutching the binoculars, he left the chair and moved quietly across the Navajo rug to the door. He laid his hand on the cool knob and yanked it open.

Billy Easter stood outside, his body crouched forward. He straightened up with a guilty look on his face.

"I told you to stay downstairs!" Mr. McGregor snapped.

Billy's eyes went from the chair drawn up to the window to the binoculars in the old man's hand. "I ran out of magazines," he said lamely.

"No, you didn't. You came up here to spy on me."

"I was just gonna knock when you opened the door."

The old man felt betrayed. His earlier suspicions were confirmed; Billy would have to be released. "Go to the car," he said.

"We're leaving?"

"Go to the car."

Billy slipped gratefully away. Mr. McGregor gathered up the box and wrappings and pushed the chair back to its former position. He inspected the large keyhole in the door. A piece of sealing tape would be necessary.

He burned the box in the brick fireplace downstairs,

watching it flare yellow and then blacken. He could hear Billy revving the Lincoln in the closed garage. The car, he knew, was going to be a problem.

That evening they drove in circles around the school. Something was going on. Automobiles filled the parking lot and people strolled the grounds before entering the building. Lights were burning in all the rooms, flooding out over the plants in the patio. Even the bell tower was illuminated by secret bulbs, the crouching angel glowing like a gigantic piece of white sugar candy.

Puzzled, Mr. McGregor finally decided they should park in the lot. Billy had been silent since the afternoon, grunting now and then to show affirmation or disapproval. Perhaps he sensed the end was coming.

A parking attendant directed them to a spot, and Mr. McGregor opened the door. "Stay here," he said, getting out.

Billy didn't answer. He pulled the peak of his chauffeur's cap over his eyes and stretched out across the front seat. Mr. McGregor felt like reprimanding him, but it would be a waste of breath. The man's habits were meaningless now.

A wave of adults was crossing the grounds toward the lit entrance way, and the old man joined them. They were mostly couples, husbands and wives, and striding along with them he felt as safe as a chameleon with his neat blue suit and respectable white hair. He was just another face on the dark lawn, perhaps a grandfather interested in school affairs.

He moved along with the others up the steps and into the building, eager to see where Tod and Amy spent their days. It was a cheerful enough place, with walls the color of surf and modern fluorescent fixtures that poured bright, antiseptic light down over the bobbing heads and shoulders in the long hall. Tacked on bulletin boards were rows of brown-paper drawings: awkward crayoned sunsets and wriggly children that looked like centipedes.

Mr. McGregor edged his way over to the far wall. Everyone seemed to have found friends, and they were talking in avid, ringing tones. He was reminded of a P.T.A. meeting that he and Loretta had attended at Mark's school in Beverly Hills. One of the mothers was a well-known film actress, and the other parents kept stealing looks at her. But she had seemed to him quite average, a plump-faced, middle-aged woman in a ski coat.

The crowd in the hall was gradually moving, as if toward the mouth of a funnel. Mr. McGregor tried to press himself to the wall but he was slowly borne along. The crayon drawings slipped past him, and he saw that people were flowing through two large doors into an auditorium. Fortunately there was a small alcove with a drinking fountain a few feet away. He bent over the fountain, pretending to drink, and the crowd filed around him. He watched the passing faces from a corner of his eye. Perhaps Dorothy, the children's mother, was among them. If so, Tod and Amy would probably be alone at home with only a thin door between them and himself. But as the last few parents trickled into the auditorium he gave up hope. Dorothy Hubbard would never attend a school meeting. She wasn't the type.

"We're ready to begin," said a soft voice at his elbow.

He jerked up from the fountain. A nun was smiling sweetly at him. She wore thin steel glasses, and there was a small mole on the side of her chin. "Just getting a drink," he mumbled.

The sister closed one of the doors and gestured at the other. "You'd better hurry," she said, still smiling. "I hope all the seats haven't been taken."

Mr. McGregor glanced down the long, polished hall toward the front door. He could turn quickly and walk out.

But her eyes held him, scolding him gently for his hesitation. If he left, she might have reason for remembering him. "Thank you, Sister," he said.

He ducked through the second door, and she closed it behind him. Dazed and disconcerted, he groped about in the rear of the room. He saw that it wasn't really an auditorium; it was more like a chapel, small and soundproofed, with a permanent altar and plaster figures of Christ and the Virgin standing out in vivid bas-relief on the far wall. All of the seats were occupied, including several rows of folding chairs that formed temporary wings on the side. Standees were clustered in the small foyer.

Mr. McGregor looked back nervously at the two closed doors. The sister with the mole was no doubt standing just outside. He felt cramped and threatened in the hushed, overheated room. Fortunately it was semi-dark; he knew that anyone observing him would only see the pale blur of his face. Suddenly one of the doors opened and the sister came in. She remained with her back to the door, looking past him toward the lit altar.

Mr. McGregor kneaded his hands. Why had he come here? Now he'd be trapped for an hour or more while Billy grew impatient in the car.

One of the sisters rose and went to the altar. She led the assemblage in a short prayer and then introduced the Mother Superior, a stout, commanding woman with a hearing aid. Mr. McGregor shifted his weight to his other foot and glanced at the door.

"Welcome," the Mother Superior said, her stolid smile turning to encompass all corners of the cramped chapel. "This is a most unexpected and gratifying turnout. I'm sorry we didn't have the foresight to provide enough chairs, but we're getting more from the basement."

Mr. McGregor perked up. In the confusion he might have a chance to slip out unobserved.

"Before we begin our meeting," the nun continued, "I have an important announcement to make. Our school bus must go into the shop tomorrow afternoon for repairs." A soft murmur ran through the room. The Mother Superior smiled indulgently. "As you suspect, we will have to make arrangements for those children who depend on this form of transportation."

The bus, the old man mused, drawn away from his problems. Tod and Amy used the bus.

"We would like to avoid any confusion tomorrow afternoon," the woman went on. "After our meeting tonight the staff and I would like to make up a list of those mothers who will be available with cars to assist us. The garage, I might add, has given its word that the bus will be ready for use the following morning."

She sipped from a glass of water and then called on a sister to make a report, but the old man wasn't listening. His mind was calculating possibilities. The children's mother wasn't at the meeting, and there was a chance she wouldn't learn about the bus. Tod and Amy would be temporarily stranded the following day after school—unless someone, a sympathetic priest, came by to pick them up. . . .

Mr. McGregor turned to the door. He couldn't afford to waste any more time. The sister with the mole was looking at him, her spectacles little coins of blank light. "I just remembered, Sister, I believe I left the lights on in my car, I'll be right back."

She nodded and stepped aside. Mr. McGregor brushed past her and hurried down the empty hall. It seemed so easy, so opportune. He had been planning to spend weeks on surveillance, and now the breakdown of a school bus had provided him with a perfect chance. He was almost laughing as he rapped on the glass next to Billy Easter's sleeping face. "Wake up!" he said.

Drowsily, Billy started the car as the old man climbed

in the back. "The house?" he asked, yawning.

"Just drive. Anywhere. I have to think."

Billy Easter gunned the car out of the lot.

The ocean streamed past the windows, reflected gray on the windshield like frost. All four windows were lowered, and the cold ocean air struck at Mr. McGregor's face, beating at his temples and depositing small drops of moisture in his heavy eyebrows. The night cold was a special tonic; he wallowed in it as if it was a reviving bath. It seemed to be blowing straight from the north, carrying bits of pine needles and balsam.

He would need a car. That was the first step, acquiring an old model that couldn't be identified and traced by the police. He opened his mouth, sucking in the wind till his tongue was ice.

Billy Easter was shivering. "Can't we close the windows?"

The old man studied his chauffeur's profile as the headlights of oncoming cars broke across his face. He knew he'd have to take Billy into his confidence, and he resented the risk, but who else could he call on for assistance? Certainly not Norman. And he couldn't very well steal a car by himself. "I need an automobile," he said, hoping a new pair of headlights would flash by so he could see Billy's expression.

"What do you think I'm driving?"

"I need another one."

"Where you gonna buy a car at this hour? It's almost midnight."

"I didn't say I wanted to buy one."

Billy Easter turned slightly.

"Watch out where you're going!"

Billy's eyes met his in the rearview mirror. "You trying

to say you're thinking of *stealing* one?"

The old man didn't answer.

"Well?"

"All I want to know is whether or not you can get me a car." He held his breath. A great deal depended on the answer.

Billy was silent as the passing lights continued to illuminate his face. "I'm supposed to go to a lot of trouble for nothing?"

Mr. McGregor relaxed. It all came down to money. "Naturally, I'd be willing to pay."

"How much?"

"Two hundred dollars."

Billy laughed. "For two-hundred bucks you expect me to hot-jump somebody's car and maybe land in jail?"

"Three-hundred."

"Five," said Billy flatly. "That's rock bottom."

The old man rolled up one of the windows. He was beginning to get an earache. "I'll need it tonight," he said.

Billy caught his eyes again in the mirror. "Let's get this straight. You're willing to pay me five-hundred dollars if I steal you a car?"

"That's correct. Is it a bargain?"

"Now hold on just one second. How come you want another car? What's wrong with this one?"

"It's a private business matter." The less he discussed it the better. By morning Billy would be gone.

"Where's the money?" The tone was sly.

The old man removed his wallet and thumbed through the bills. "I'll give you half now. But I don't have it with me. We'll have to drive back to the house."

"I don't want no down payment. I want it all."

"Don't be ridiculous. You'll get the rest when you bring me the car."

THE PLAYHOUSE

Billy grunted his disapproval, but the old man noticed that he was maneuvering the car into the left lane for a U turn. Horns sounded behind them. Mr. McGregor rested his face against the seat cushions, the cold wind stirring his hair. The pain in his ear had increased. It was like a small, burning hook in his head.

"Five hundred," Billy Easter reminded him, seeking confirmation. "Not a penny less."

"That was the deal," said Mr. McGregor.

The old man ordered Billy to stay in the kitchen.

"I don't care *where* you keep your money," Billy grumbled through the closed door.

"I won't be long," Mr. McGregor assured him.

He tramped his feet on the stairs, pretending to climb them, then he moved on tiptoe across the living room toward the built-in bar. He knew Billy was aware a safe was hidden in the house, but he had never found the exact location.

Skipper growled at his trouser cuff as he moved the bottles aside and opened the panel built into the wooden shelving. "Go away," he whispered. But Skipper remained near his feet, looking up at him with sad, confused eyes.

Mr. McGregor set the numerals on the metal wheels of the small safe. Moonlight brushed the backs of his fluttering hands and stained them with leaf shadows from the window. He suddenly thought he saw the little people peering into the room, watching and commenting while he went through the contents of the safe. Disturbed, he pulled the curtains, shutting out the shadows and the whispering night leaves.

The safe was crammed with stacks of securities and a large amount of cash. Mr. McGregor removed four fifties and three hundreds. He placed them in his wallet, closed the safe, and shut the panel. After pounding his feet on the stairway again, he went back to the kitchen and opened the door.

"It's somewhere in the living room," said Billy Easter, grinning. He had made himself a liverwurst sandwich from the refrigerator. "You banged your feet on the stairs but you didn't really go up."

Mr. McGregor glared at him. It was going to be a relief living by himself again. He counted two-hundred and fifty dollars on the kitchen table. A few of his cats walked around the stack of currency, one of them touching it tentatively with an amber paw. Billy looked at the money, then he scooped it up, holding it briefly to his nose. "Smells like camphor," he said.

Mr. McGregor checked his pocket watch. "How long will it take you?"

Billy shrugged. "Few hours. Might have to go downtown and shop around."

"Be careful."

"That's what you're paying me for."

Mr. McGregor felt light-headed. It had actually begun.

Billy went to the kitchen door, still nibbling on the sandwich. "I guess you'll be up when I get back."

Mr. McGregor nodded. He sat down at the table and one of the cats rolled like a tiny silk ball into his lap. He scratched it behind the skull; it was like a little child, warm and nervous.

"The key," said Billy. "I can't drive that Lincoln over the gate."

The old man reluctantly took the shoestring from around his neck and held it out. Billy took it and tossed the rind of his sandwich into the sink. "I won't be long," he said, slipping out into the yard.

Mr. McGregor heard the garage door open and then, a

few minutes later, the clanging of the gates. Still holding the little cat, he rose and went to the window. The playhouse loomed on the lawn, its windows wet with starlight, its painted prow poised for voyage. It wouldn't be empty much longer, he thought.

Billy Easter drove through the downtown section of the city. It was late, yet the streets were full of automobiles. Their chrome parts winked in the moonlight, inviting his secret inspection, but he had no intention of stealing a car. That was a felony, and sooner or later a big blue arm would be dangling a pair of handcuffs at him. He shook his head with wonder. Old McGregor must think everyone else was crazy, too.

When he reached his destination the garage was dark. He frowned. Felix, or at least one of his men, was always around, twenty-four hours a day. He parked on the cement apron outside the tall, corrugated steel door and rang the night bell. Almost immediately a slat opened and a Mexican he had seen before looked out.

"It's me. Billy Easter. Is Felix here?"

The Mexican nodded, and a moment later the steel door rose electronically so Billy could enter. Inside, the garage was a rectangle of flat yellow light. A mechanic in overalls was spraying a powder-blue car with green paint and another workman was hammering a crumpled fender. The room seemed to echo, rattling the dusty panes in the overhead skylight.

The Mexican indicated a glassed-in office half-hidden by a row of coffee and soda machines. Billy had been there once before; it was Felix's private den where he tore furiously through his paperwork and sometimes slept on an army cot. He walked toward it, savoring the importance of his position and the feel of the wad of money wrapped around his bone.

Felix was sitting behind his desk. He was a middle-aged Mexican with a brown, bulging face like a handmade cigarette. He was wearing a Hawaiian sportshirt tucked loosely into cotton trousers. His face darkened when he looked up. "I'm busy."

Billy was usually intimidated by this sulky, powerful man whose activities were something of a legend in the neighborhood. But he crossed to the desk and smiled confidently. "I need a car," he said.

"Take a bus. It's cheaper."

"I got money." Billy unfurled a bill and laid it on the desk.

The Mexican puffed out his cheeks and blew it across the blotter. "That's just about enough to get you some gasoline for a motor scooter."

Billy put another bill beside it. "Don't want a Cadillac," he said. "Just something that runs."

Felix gathered up the money. "Seems to me the last time I saw you your tail was dragging."

"I got lucky."

The Mexican studied him with a slightly bored, slightly amused expression. He stuck a small brown cigar in the corner of his mouth and rose languidly from behind the desk. Billy followed him through a door that led to the area behind the garage. He had never seen the yard before. Surrounded by the old brick walls of the adjoining buildings, it was carpeted with a rubble of tires, twisted pieces of metal, and a litter of battered automobiles. "Take your pick," said Felix. The money had disappeared into the pocket of his shirt.

Billy poked around the debris. There were six cars, most

in an advanced state of deterioration. One, however, an old Chevrolet coupe, seemed in better condition than the rest. Its paint was scratched but still respectable and the treads on the tires were only partially worn.

"We picked up a real beauty tonight," said Felix. "Brand-new Pontiac. I'll let you have it for twelve-fifty."

Billy didn't reply. He kicked the tires on the Chevy and lifted the hood.

"That's a rattle trap," Felix said derisively. "Let me show you the Pontiac. They're putting on a new coat of paint."

Billy was pleased, but he tried not to show it. Too much interest would cost money. "You got a key for this sorry sight?" he asked.

"In the ignition. You got all the taste of a jaybird."

Billy started the motor, climbed out, and watched the activity under the hood. Everything ran smoothly except for the fan belt, which obviously needed a replacement. But that was the old man's problem. "It might do," he said eventually. "I don't know."

"Tell you what. Estaban says you've been driving a Lincoln for the guy you work for. Maybe we can make a trade for the Pontiac. You can say the Lincoln was stolen."

"No deal." Billy got behind the wheel again. There was the smell of rust somewhere, but it didn't matter.

"Drive this crate home," Felix said, "and your wife will throw up."

"You got a chain?"

Felix stared at him, removing the cigar from his mouth. "A tow chain? Where you planning on hauling this heap?"

Billy gave him a white grin. "To a friend's." He enjoyed puzzling the Mexican. For the first time since he could remember he was one up on him. "Why should it matter? It's not that maybe this is a hot car, is it?"

"Do I look worried?" the Mexican asked. "Tell Estaban

I said it's okay to give you a chain. And watch yourself, amigo. Looks to me like you're thinking of pulling something."

Billy felt flattered. "Could be," he said. "Hang on to that Pontiac. I might be buying it one of these days."

Felix walked slowly back toward the garage. "I doubt it," he called back over his shoulder. "From this angle, I doubt it."

The door slammed. Billy knew he had been slighted, but someday he *would* buy one of Felix's cars, one of the fine ones. He headed for the garage to find Estaban.

Mr. McGregor hesitated, clearing his throat. They were standing in the garage of the rented house where Billy had parked the two cars. The only light came from a hundred-watt bulb, ringed by wire meshing, that shone harshly on the rough cinder-block walls.

"Maybe I didn't hear you right," said Billy.

"I simply said that I won't be needing you anymore," the old man repeated.

"Look, I know you're still mad at me from this afternoon. I *was* sort of spying on you. But I won't do it again."

"It has nothing to do with that."

"You don't like the car I got you?"

Mr. McGregor wished he could be more detached. "I just don't need your services any longer, Billy. Nothing personal. I'm thinking of selling the house and moving to a much smaller place."

Billy stuffed his hands in his pockets. "I don't believe you."

"It happens to be the truth. I've talked the whole thing over with Norman, and he agrees with me. I'll go into one of those new co-ops on Wilshire Boulevard."

"Who's gonna drive you around?"

"No one. If I have to go out, I'll take a taxi."

Billy came closer. The light was directly behind him, and his face was in darkness. "Why so awful sudden?" he asked. "Why can't I stay till tomorrow?"

"It's a business matter."

"I don't see no business. All you've been doing is following them kids around and watching that school."

Mr. McGregor removed a wad of bills from his pocket. "I realize this is short notice," he said.

"Damn right. The last guy I worked for gave me two weeks."

The old man laid out the money on the hood of the Chevrolet. Eight one-hundred-dollar bills.

"That's supposed to make everything okay?"

"It's a gift."

Billy glanced at the bills. Mr. McGregor wondered if he could make out the denominations. Perhaps he didn't realize how much was there.

"Hey," said Billy, "suppose I take a vacation for a couple of weeks, come back after you're in the new place?"

The old man shook his head. "I don't need anyone anymore."

Billy banged his hands against his thighs. "What am I gonna do for references? You didn't even write me a letter."

"Have them call. I'll say you were an excellent chauffeur."

Billy walked around the side of the car, turning his back on the money. "You know what you're doing?" he said. "You're firing me." He snapped his fingers. "Just like that. So long, Billy Easter. Fly away."

"I'm not firing you. I'm letting you go."

Billy swung around again. "Why can't I wait till tomorrow? Give me one good reason."

Mr. McGregor reached in back of the Lincoln and removed a leather traveling bag.

"What's that?"

"Your things. I took the liberty of packing them while you were out getting the car."

Billy's eyes widened. He didn't seem angry any longer, just perplexed. "You packed my stuff?"

"I wanted to save you the trouble." Mr. McGregor didn't wish to appear callous. After all, the man had been loyal to him and certain of his annoying traits aside, he rather liked him.

"Just like that," Billy Easter marveled. "One, two, three—go find another job."

The old man placed the traveling bag down on the oil-stained floor. It seemed so light. Billy had been with him almost two years, and he had collected no more possessions than a sparrow.

"Everything in there?" Billy asked.

"Everything I could find. You can keep the bag."

"Thanks." The word was abrupt.

I can still change my mind, Mr. McGregor thought. But tomorrow at the school someone might remember the two of them, especially since one was black. No, the risk was too great.

Billy picked up the money. He held it for a moment in his broad dark hand, then swept the stack into his trouser pocket. He picked up the bag and reached out to stroke Skipper's ears.

"Please call me if you need a reference," Mr. McGregor said.

Billy nodded. He went to the garage door, lifted it, and walked slowly toward the lawn.

Mr. McGregor ran to the door. "Billy..." he called. "Goodbye."

But Billy didn't turn back. He was already halfway down the slope to the street. Soon he had merged with the trees, and then he was only a shadow.

The old man looked after him, surprised that Billy's departure had produced an unexpected loneliness instead of relief. Now the chauffeur had joined all the others: his wife, Loretta, the children. And here he was in someone else's garage, with someone else's car, planning to take someone else's son and daughter. Sadly, he went into the house.

He sat in the bright kitchen looking at the remains of Billy's afternoon sandwich and the discarded magazines. Skipper prowled at his feet, picking at a piece of broken tile, acutely aware of the alien house.

After a while Mr. McGregor took a pint brandy bottle from his inside jacket pocket and poured some of the liquor into the gold cap. It smelled strong and tart, but he looked upon it as a medicine. In a few minutes he would have to go out to the stolen car and drive it along the street. The thought paralyzed him; the more he turned it over in his mind, the more frightened he became. Ever since the accident he had been unable to bear sitting in the front seat of an automobile. Even in the back he sometimes felt a choking feeling much like the one he dreaded at the sanitarium.

He downed the drink, and it went glowing through his body, spreading out like warm smoke. Then he tipped the bottle to his lips and drank deeply for as long as he could. It nauseated him. He tore the bottle away, his gums stinging. There was still no reaction, just the warmth in his stomach and legs. Skipper was watching him from under the kitchen table. "Do you want to see me get drunk, Skipper boy?" he muttered.

He took another drink. Now he detected a subtle change; the ceiling light seemed brighter, and he was more aware of the objects around him, the curtains on the window, the plastic salt and pepper shakers lined up like toy soldiers. But when he thought of the waiting car he was seized again by the feeling of paralysis.

More brandy. Some of it spilled, and Skipper crept back under the table. Mr. McGregor wiped his raw, wet mouth and lurched around the kitchen, furious with himself. He'd simply have to force his legs to take him to the car. He'd get inside and close the door and conquer this insane panic. Determined, he stumbled toward the garage. Skipper barked at his heels.

"Be quiet!" he commanded. "Do you want to wake the neighbors?"

He entered the garage and studied the car. Its windows were open like an invitation. Mr. McGregor's fingers smeared the accumulated dust on the body. He closed his eyes and jerked open the door. It was musty inside, the smell of cheap, acrid seat covers, and he sneezed twice violently. Open your eyes, he told himself. There's nothing here that's going to hurt you.

He slumped down on the seat. Grasping the steering wheel, he brought himself into a sitting position. His mouth seemed dry, smothered. It was almost like being propped up in a coffin. He couldn't quite bring himself to close the door—it would only intensify the feeling. But how could he possibly drive with the door open?

Give it time, he thought. Just rest behind the wheel. He closed his eyes and had the acute sense that he was losing his balance. He opened them quickly, grasping the wheel with both hands, hanging on. "Skipper!" he called. "Get in here."

The dog was plainly confused, but Mr. McGregor reached out, grabbed it by the collar, and pulled it over his lap onto the other side of the seat. "Stay here," he said. He looked through the windshield at the rough slabs of cinder block and nervously stroked Skipper's thick coat. Relax, he thought, relax. Perhaps he needed fresh air; if he could take the car out into the clean night, he'd feel better.

How did these things work? He remembered the old days when he'd climb into a car without a second thought. Why wouldn't the motions come back to him? First—it was really so laughably simple—you turned on the ignition key and shifted the gear into neutral. Was this one automatic? Yes. Good. He pressed the gas pedal down slightly and the motor kicked over, went dead. He tried again, and the motor caught. The entire car vibrated heavily, the wheel tingling under his tense fingers.

Now—he had to back out of the garage without hitting the Lincoln that was parked only inches away. The reverse gear. Put the car in reverse. The gear was stuck. He frantically shifted back into drive and neutral, but it wouldn't go forward into reverse. The damn old car. Why didn't Billy have the good sense to steal a new one? He tried again, pumping the brake at the same time. Miraculously, as if the two were somehow connected, he was able to ease the gear into reverse.

He rubbed his sleeve over his forehead. What was next? He had to back the car past the limousine and out onto the drive. The motor was still idling, and he kept a small, steady pressure on the gas so it wouldn't stall.

Holding his breath, he gently tapped the pedal. Nothing happened. The car didn't move. What was wrong now? Had Billy brought him a lemon? He took a chance, floored the accelerator, and the motor boomed hollowly under the hood, but they were still rooted to the same spot.

Mr. McGregor sagged, defeated, his eyes blurred with perspiration. It was all too much. He should have kept Billy and taken his chances. Then he laughed. The hand brake. He had forgotten the hand brake. What a fool!

Skipper started barking as he slowly, foot by foot, backed

the car out of the garage. But he hadn't counted on the steep driveway. Suddenly he was rolling backwards, much too fast, heading for the lawn of the opposite house. He pumped the brake in panic but the rear wheels struck the curb and spun the little vehicle around like a twig. They stopped, stalled, in the middle of the road while Skipper lunged at the window, still barking.

A car was coming down the street. Its headlights filled Mr. McGregor's eyes; everything was suddenly as bright as noon. He held his breath. Was there room to pass? Would the driver pause to see if he needed assistance? Even worse, could it be a neighborhood patrol car? He felt as helpless as a turtle on its back. The other vehicle flicked its brights at him; it was almost as if he was being photographed.

The car came abreast, then pulled around him and continued on its way, indifferent. A few moments later its taillights vanished down the street. Mr. McGregor didn't move. He was exhausted and he thought how nice it would be to go to sleep. A mailman would find him in the morning, parked at an impossible angle, and perhaps wake him with a cold glass of orange juice.

Skipper had begun to whimper. Mr. McGregor looked up apprehensively at the surrounding houses. They were dark and remote, as silent as their gardens. He stroked the dog until it calmed down and then started the motor again. Carefully, with a growing sense of power, he drove around the block, reacquainting himself with the delicate arts of judging distance and braking before a stop. Skipper seemed to sense his confidence and settled down quietly on the seat. The old man, still braced with brandy, was delighted. It was like riding a bike or taking a swim after years of abstinence; the mind and the reflexes never quite forgot.

He drove back to the house and steered the car into the garage. Skipper was dozing. It was all over, and he could hardly keep his eyes open. He let his head fall forward on the wheel, his mouth whispering against the edge of the horn. It suddenly seemed that he was in his own bed, cuddling a strange metal pillow. Soon the strangeness had left him, and he had retreated into sleep.

Sister Mary Catherine inspected the school window. It was smudged with spiderwebs of dirt that began in the center and radiated out toward the corners. The sun hung in the strands, turning the glass into an orange smear that was almost opaque. She scowled; the window hadn't been cleaned in a week, and the children were deprived of the view outside. She turned, her hands on her hips, and looked down the hall.

Mr. Fosse, one of the janitor's assistants, was mopping the tile floor near the entrance doors, leaving a broad wake of foam behind him. It was almost the end of the school day, and he was starting his clean-up duties early. "Mr. Fosse," she called, "could you spare me a minute, please?"

He left the mop in his bucket and approached her with a wary look on his tanned face.

"This window hasn't been cleaned in centuries," she said, tilting her steel-rimmed spectacles so she could see him better.

"I just get the floors," he mumbled. "McIllhenny does the windows, Sister. That's McIllhenny's job."

"Mr. McIllhenny's on the lawn this week," she said, convinced that he already knew. "Would it be too much for you to get a bottle of Windex and a cloth?"

"I got to finish the floor."

"I'm sure you can make room in your schedule." She had the unpleasant feeling that he was focusing his disrespect on the little mole on her chin.

He twisted his red hands. "Okay, I'll get the window. The floor'll have to wait."

"Thank you."

After he had gone to get his cleaning equipment, Sister Mary Catherine glanced again at the offending window. It was filthy, alive with dirt and the whorls of thumb marks. She would have to report Mr. McIllhenny to the Mother Superior. No—that would be too strong a measure. She'd talk to the man himself.

Mr. Fosse returned and grumpily sprayed some blue liquid on the pane. Classes were over now, and children thronged the hall, squirming their way through the two main exits. Sister Mary Catherine stayed by the window, silently supervising the cleaning. She said nothing to Mr. Fosse as he rubbed and polished a transparent swathe in the glass. She looked through the cleared area as it gradually increased in size and saw the front rim of the lawn where a dozen or more cars were parked. The school bus was being repaired, and the parents had formed a pool to pick up their children. Little boys and girls were swooping and hooting, enjoying the rupture of their normal schedule, while mothers moved among them trying to find their youngsters. Strange, the Sister thought. There was a man among them, a stubby white-haired priest who stood isolated near an old car. She knew most of the priests in the community, but she had never seen this one before. There was, however, something vaguely familiar about his face. He seemed tense and secretive as his gaze swept over the children. He appeared to be hunting like the mothers, but there was a strained expression in his eyes. Perhaps he was looking at the sun.

"How's that?" Mr. Fosse asked, stepping back.

She nodded, hardly listening. The priest absorbed her attention. Now he was moving with a slow, hesitant stride, his eyes still roaming. He was no taller than some of the upper-class boys, and she had the odd feeling that he was a child too, dressed up as a priest for Halloween. But then his white head dwarfed a flock of little girls, and he was a grown man again.

"You oughta lay the law down to McIllhenny, Sister. He's been getting away with murder around here." Mr. Fosse slipped the bottle of Windex into the pocket of his overalls.

Who was he, and where had she seen him? As Mr. Fosse moved away she forced herself to concentrate. It had been recently, sometime within the past week. Her memory seemed to itch as she hovered on the tip of recognition. She stared at his face, very white over his dusty black suit. Last night! She had seen him last night. But was it after school, at the parents meeting, or in the drugstore where she had joined the other sisters for plates of lemon sherbet? A priest. Where could she have seen a strange priest who didn't belong in the community?

Most of the children were gone now, swept into the waiting cars that were pulling away down the drive. The priest was still there, his eyes more eager than ever. The sun had dipped lower, slanting through the trees and stretching his shadow across the beautiful lawn. Now he was very still, his hands lost in his pockets. He was looking toward the building, and Sister Mary Catherine ducked away from the window. She knew she was acting foolishly, but she didn't want to meet his eyes.

Mr. McIllhenny entered the building. He was dressed in khakis, and bits and pieces of grass clung to his shoes. Sister Mary Catherine called to him, suddenly reminded of the dirty window and his lack of responsibility. In an instant she had forgotten the priest. "Mr. McIllhenny," she said, tilting her spectacles, "I'd like to have a word with you."

* * *

Mr. McGregor walked in small, choppy circles, his finger-nails digging into his damp palms, his heels wearing ruts in the lawn. The sun was warm on his back, like the hand of a friend, and he was sweating in the heavy suit. His pocket watch ticked on his stomach; he was afraid to take it out and look at the time. What was keeping them? Where were they?

A few children wandered from the building, some walking home, he imagined, others heading for the boulevard to take the public bus, but Tod and Amy were still inside, struggling over their lessons or perhaps kept after school. The cars and parents were gone, and he realized that he was conspicuous in his clerical collar. Suppose a nun came out and started asking questions? She'd catch him in a lie, and he would have to run to the car and drive away. The suit began to itch, and he could feel a heat rash spreading slowly over his shoulders. Why didn't they come?

A man in kahkis, probably a janitor, left the building and came toward him. His face was an angry cherry-red, and he glanced ferociously at Mr. McGregor as he strode past, his feet kicking at stones. Does he know me? the old man wondered. Why did he give me that threatening look? But the janitor crossed to a power lawn mower and climbed up on its seat. He drove the machine off in a crazy, zig-zag pattern.

Mr. McGregor was digging in his pocket for his watch when he saw the wooden door swing open at the entrance. Several nuns came out and began walking down the path in his direction. Should he turn and hide in the car until they had passed? It was too late. He could feel their innocent gaze touch him as they strolled by. "Afternoon, Father," they chirped.

"Afternoon," he mumbled, his eyes on the grass. They went down the road in a rustle of robes.

Four o'clock. Drops of sweat sat on his forehead like

boils. He knew he couldn't wait much longer; it was a physical impossibility. If only Billy were still with him, hunched in the car over his inevitable newspaper.

He turned around, disconsolate, and almost bumped into Tod. The boy had come running from behind the building, moving through the silky grass. Amy was with him, carrying their school books.

Mr. McGregor steadied himself and tried to smile. The boy was watching him with heavy-lidded, suspicious eyes. "Hello, son," he said, clearing his throat. His voice sounded dry and dead.

The boy didn't answer. His sister came up and leaned against him.

"I've come to take you home," he said, forcing warmth into his voice. "The bus won't be ready until tomorrow," he added inanely.

"Look," the girl said, showing him her elbow. It was crusted with a small brown scab. "It's all better now."

Mr. McGregor swallowed. She remembered him. But did they question his clerical clothing?

The boy squatted and picked up a white stone. "You want to take us home?"

"Yes. Your mother's at work, and she doesn't have time to pick you up."

The girl started to say something but Tod interrupted her. "That your car?" he asked.

The old man nodded. "Come along," he said firmly. He put his hand on Tod's shoulder but the boy spun away. Amy sat down on the lawn and tried to balance the books on her head.

"You talked to Mom?" Tod asked. He held the stone at arm's length, and the sun twinkled on its mica edges.

"Yes. I told you she's at work."

The books slid from Amy's head and landed in the grass. "I don't like your car," she said to him. "It's all dirty."

"But it rides nicely," he assured her. It was like talking to Ruthie, picking his way through the maze of a child's logic.

"Do you know where we live?" Tod said. He was standing very straight now, his head tilted at an odd angle as if the old man was a teacher or a soldier.

"You can give me instructions. I'm sure it won't be hard to find."

"Does your car have power steering?" the little girl asked.

"Keep quiet," snapped the boy.

She squinted at him and made bright bubbles of saliva on her lips.

"Let's go," Mr. McGregor said. "You'll want to be there by the time your mother comes home."

"Mom!" Amy shouted.

The old man realized that she was staring past him. He looked quickly around. A car was coming toward the school from the street, a green convertible with a crumpled fender.

"Mom, mom, mom!" Amy jumped up and down and waved at the approaching car.

"That's our mother," said the boy.

Mr. McGregor was dumbfounded. One of the nuns must have told her, called the house. And Tod knew she was coming all along. He had played a trick on him.

The convertible parked behind the car, and Dorothy Hubbard got out. She wore a thin silk dress with a gold belt. "In we go, monsters," she called. Her eyes were masked by sunglasses, and the old man couldn't tell if she noticed him.

Tod sailed his stone into the air and walked over to his mother. The little girl gathered up the books and brushed the grass from her skirt with a fussy gesture. "We have an old car, too," she explained to Mr. McGregor. "But ours has power steering."

She skipped across to the car and tumbled into the front seat with her brother. The woman got in beside them. The old man watched as the car turned in the parking area and went rattling down the road. He wasn't sure, it might have been a trick of the fading sunlight, but it seemed as if the children were waving to him from the window. Then the car joined the traffic on the boulevard and he was alone, standing there under the gaze of the white-sugar angel.

He didn't eat dinner that night. He roamed the house on the edge of tears, followed by the dog, and drank cheap wine right from the bottle. No one had fed the cats, and they mewed in the big dark kitchen. The Swiss clock chimed the hours, and still he rambled through the empty halls, his collar unbuttoned, his feet in carpet slippers. His mind was numb. The whole plan had been a mistake, a dream. By habit he checked the doors and windows. There was a dry wind outside, prowling the estate like a trespasser. It rattled the panes and shook dead branches down the walls, swirling the dust of logs in the fireplace.

The telephone rang. Mr. McGregor almost dropped the wine bottle. It was a sound totally unexpected, and he listened to the long, shrill rings with an expression of amazement. It continued to ring, driving the kittens from the kitchen, and he cupped his cold hands to his ears. Perhaps it was someone playing a practical joke, dialing numbers at random from the directory. He wouldn't pick it up; it would have to spend itself. Finally the ringing stopped, and the old man felt relieved. It was probably Norman, calling to set up a luncheon appointment.

Later in the night he realized that he would have to leave the house. It would be impossible to sleep there—he was afraid of entering a room and finding Loretta peeling an orange or Mark and Ruthie dragging their trains along the carpet. The house held ghosts, and he felt with a strange tenderness that he should allow them to wander in peace.

He took Skipper along for company and drove the coupe back to the colonial house on the hill. Exhausted, he climbed the stairs to the master bedroom, pulled the chair close to the window, and sat down. There was a wind here too, but it was a safe wind. It shivered the bell in the school tower, creating formless notes that were oddly soothing. He pressed his check against the warm headrest. His bladder ached but he was too tired to find the bathroom. Skipper nuzzled the palm of his hand and soon the bell was tolling somewhere inside his dreams.

He woke on the following noon to the sound of children's voices. For a moment he was a child himself, squatting with the neighborhood rabble in the dirt outside his father's store. It was twilight, and he had wet his pants. But when he opened his eyes they were filled with sunlight. It poured through the room, winking on the discarded field glasses and sparkling on the fibers of the Navajo rug. Skipper was asleep beside him. He was afraid to move. His head felt hollow from the wine, a burst balloon. His mouth and lips were dry.

Far below, past the green of the trees, the playground was teeming with children. He was fascinated by the darting circles and patterns they made. He closed his eyes and fancied he could feel their shadows moving across his lids. Perhaps Tod and Amy were down there. It was just another school day for them; he was sure they had forgotten the incident at the car. He reached over the edge of the chair and retrieved the binoculars, all the long muscles in his arm aching. Skipper rose and growled.

The binoculars seemed heavier than he remembered. He brought them to his eyes and adjusted the lenses. Faces sprang up, magnified like soap bubbles. There was the nun with the steel-rimmed spectacles who had guarded the door at the meeting. She was holding a little boy up to the drinking fountain, tilting his face into the spray. The jungle gym was in the background, and he hastily moved the glasses to another section of the yard. Perhaps he could find the group of boys playing with their paper squares. He scanned the concrete, but he couldn't locate the game.

Tod! There he was, standing at the edge of the yard. There was furious activity all around him, but he made no effort to participate. Mr. McGregor moved the glasses in a circle, hunting for Amy. She wasn't with him, and he decided that her recess period was probably later in the day. He concentrated again on the boy. From a distance the similarity was amazing: Tod-Mark isolated from the group, picking over his private thoughts. If only Loretta could see him.

Gone! The old man jiggled the lenses. It was exactly like the first time—he had been there one moment and vanished the next. He went slowly over the yard where the boy had stood, searching for holes or obstructions. It was impossible. He had to be somewhere in the playground.

He lowered the field glasses and rubbed his eyes. His mind was playing tricks again. He looked up and then moved closer to the window, the binoculars forgotten. There was a dark-blue blur moving through the trees that separated the school grounds from the road. Yes—it was Tod, running low through the grass. He must have ducked down so the others wouldn't see him and headed for the patch of trees. But why, and where was he going?

Hands sweating, he raised the binoculars again. The boy was running more slowly now, his body part of the dark leaves. The face flashed with sunlight, the skin very pale, then disappeared.

Mr. McGregor dropped the glasses and stumbled toward the open door. His legs felt heavy, almost useless. Skipper frisked behind him. "Stay here!" he shouted. "Don't come along."

Down the carpeted stairs, the blood rushing to his head. The boy was alone. Maybe there was still a chance to take him, the sister later. Stay there, he prayed. Stay there till I come.

The sunlight stunned him for a dizzy moment as he hurried across the lawn to the road, tucking his rumpled shirt inside his trousers. He knew he looked absurd. A white-haired old man on an urgent errand, smelling of sleep and wine. He brushed at his matted hair, combing the tangled strands with his fingers. A maid was hanging wash in the neighboring yard. She looked at him over the flapping clothing and then leaned on the line, her face creased with curiosity. She'll remember me, he thought.

A car coming up the street honked its horn. He dodged it, feeling its close, cool shadow on his back. It tore off, its driver shouting something. Damn, he thought. Someone else to remember him.

The trees loomed up, their branches screening the hot sun. Through the chinks in the leaves he could see the children in the playground. He paused for a moment and tried to get his breath. The trees gave off a slight dampness, a feeling of water and night, and he was glad to be out of the sun. The sounds from the playground seemed to surround him, as if the voices were pulling mischievously at his ears.

An almost invisible path led through the narrow grove, and he followed it. Away from the window and his field glasses, he had lost his sense of direction. Leaves brushed his face. He welcomed their rubbery coolness. From overhead came the drone of a plane. He listened for a moment, trying to detect another sound. Someone was crying, a child, from somewhere within the heart of the grove. It was a soft, sad sound, and it touched him with its loneliness. He followed the thin thread, moving off the path and making his way to a small cluster of weather-beaten orange crates that formed a rough circle around an oak. The crying came from behind them.

"Tod?" he called gently.

The sound stopped abruptly, but he could hear the surprised trickle of someone breathing. He pulled away one of the boxes and entered a hollowed-out space in the tangle of bushes. The boy was sitting on a stump, his foot digging furrows in the soft, mossy ground. He glanced up, more ashamed than frightened, as the old man came toward him.

"What's the matter, son?"

The boy had a small piece of paper in his fist. At first he thought it might be one of the scraps from the game. But there was something written on it; he could see sentences scrawled in violet ink. The boy stuffed it in his pocket and turned away.

Mr. McGregor studied him. The shoulders were bent brooding, just like Mark's after a scolding. "What's wrong?" he asked.

Tod looked around at him. The tears were rolling down his face, but he ignored them. "What are you doing here?"

"I want you to come with me."

The boy thought about this. He wasn't startled or perplexed; he seemed to be giving the statement his serious consideration. "Where'd you come from?" he asked.

"I've been watching you and your sister."

The boy wiped his face with a dirty hand. His cap had fallen off and lay half-buried in leaves on the ground.

"Where's Amy?" Mr. McGregor asked. He was no longer

nervous; for some strange reason he felt confident.

"In class."

"Can you bring her here? At recess?"

Tod brushed leaves from his jacket, then bent down and retrieved his cap. He turned it over and examined the stitching.

"Well?" Mr. McGregor prodded. "Can you bring her here?"

"I guess so."

The old man breathed deeply with relief. "Does anyone else know about this—little fort?"

"No," said the boy. "It's mine. I built it."

"It's very nice."

He put on his cap, backwards. "It's all right."

Mr. McGregor couldn't be sure, but the voices from the playground seemed to have receded. "When is your sister's recess period?"

"After mine."

"Will they miss you if you don't go to your next class?"

"Not for a while." He stood up.

"Tod—you'll come back with her, won't you?"

The boy nodded.

"Promise me that. I'll be waiting right here."

Tod slipped past the barricade of crates, and the old man watched him go off through the trees. Then there was a long period of silence. No wind, not even the sound of a car from the road.

Mr. McGregor sat down on the stump and held his hot head in his hands. "Give him luck," he said to himself. "Let him find his sister and come back here."

He wasn't sure how many minutes had passed, and he didn't dare look at his watch. The silence was eventually broken by the cries of children again, the second recess period. Mr. McGregor listened, holding his head and rocking back and forth on the uncomfortable stump. He thought of Loretta in her crib and the peaceful line of his wife's throat.

They weren't coming.

He hugged his knees through the heavy trousers. He couldn't remember when he had stopped praying. It was shortly after the accident, when his head began to hurt at night, and he saw the little faces at the edge of the estate. Perhaps it was a habit he could revive, like learning to drive again. Perhaps if just this once he clasped his fingers together, bit his lips, and remembered a rusty prayer. . . .

The children entered the little hollow. They came single-file, Amy holding her brother's hand. The light was behind them, like a roar of candles, and they didn't seem quite real. He looked up at them, trying to smile, trying to show them how grateful he was.

They were quiet for a while, then Amy fidgeted and broke her brother's grip. "Where's your car?" she asked.

"Nearby," he said. "Did anyone see you come?"

"No," said Tod.

He rose slowly and held out his hand to the little girl. She reached out and took it automatically. "Come along with me. We're going up to the first house on the hill."

"Is that where you live?" asked Amy.

"No," he said, pleased with her interest. "I live in the biggest house in the world. I'm sure you're going to like it there."

The girl giggled. "I don't believe you."

"Wait and see. There are so many rooms, you'll get lost in them."

Amy looked at him from a corner of her eye. "Are there any toys in your house?"

The old man nodded. "And dolls. And a dog. His name is Skipper. You'll like him, too."

Tod was studying the ground. "What about TV?" he asked.

"I'll buy one," the old man promised. "Two, if you like."

"When can we see your house?" the little girl asked, swinging his arm with hers.

"Now," said Mr. McGregor, barely able to wait himself.

PART TWO

The Holiday

"I took a corkscrew from the shelf:
I went to wake them up myself.
And when I found the door was locked,
I pulled and pushed and kicked and knocked,
And when I found the door was shut,
I tried to turn the handle, but—"

—*Through the Looking Glass*

"Good morning!" said Mr. McGregor, throwing open the curtains. "I've brought you both some fresh orange juice."

The children had slept in one of the upstairs bedrooms under an old wool blanket bright with patches and the crazy zig-zag of thread. He had looked in on them while they were still sleeping, Amy's mouth open in a wondrous 'O', the boy lying on his stomach. Even after he had flooded the room with sunlight they hardly stirred. Marveling, the old man pulled away the blanket and tickled Amy's toe.

"I don't like orange juice," she said, rolling away from the light and rubbing her eyes.

"You'll like this," he assured her. "Four oranges to the glass, and it's good and cold." He left the pitcher on the bureau and went to the door. The boy was examining the ceiling, trying to adjust himself to the strange room. "I hope you both slept well," Mr. McGregor said, jingling coins in his pocket. "I'm sure you're going to be happy here."

Later, while he scrambled eggs in the kitchen, he could hear them padding around upstairs, the sound of running water in the bathroom. There were no available toothbrushes, and he had given them a tall blue container of Morton's salt, instructing them to rub their teeth with it and rinse with cold water.

By the time they had come downstairs, waking the kittens, he had almost compiled a shopping list: clothes, underwear, toothbrushes, Crest, shoes, stockings, thermometer, bandages, milk, chocolate-chip cookies, Wheatina—everything, in fact, that he remembered as being indispensable to his grandchildren. It was like selecting provisions for a desert island, and he chuckled to himself as he added: Ex-Lax and wild cherry cough syrup.

Tod ate a hearty breakfast, his face cupped in his palm, his red-rimmed eyes still stuck together with tiny slivers of sleep. Amy jabbed at her eggs, her attention fixed on the brood of kittens that scampered around her bare ankles.

"Why aren't you drinking your milk?" he asked her.

"We're used to chocolate milk at home," she replied. She met his gaze with a silent reprimand, as if he had been careless to neglect it.

Nestlé's Chocolate, he added to the list.

When they finished their breakfast he sent them upstairs again to dress, promising that they would have an all-new wardrobe later in the day. They greeted the news with boredom.

It was a beautiful morning, a great vast sky with bursts of clouds. Mr. McGregor strolled about the grounds, puffing on a panatela, inspecting the gnawing jungle of lawn that threatened to grow to the house and sweep up its walls, turning it into a troll's castle stitched from grass. Something would have to be done, but he didn't relish summoning a troop of inquisitive gardeners to the estate.

He ended his walk at the playhouse. The dry air was still baking off the night dew, and the colors grew brighter as he watched. He waited until it was no longer wet and then trooped up on the captain's bridge and adjusted the toy barometer. "Hey up there!" he called to the closed window of the bedroom.

Tod's face stared down at him. An instant later Amy brushed him aside, and two pairs of eyes rolled over the little ship. It floated on the grass, at anchor; at any moment it seemed possible that it might set sail across the lawn, navigating among the bordering trees as if they were icebergs. Amy clapped her hands. "Can we go inside?" she asked.

"Of course. Come down. I'll show it to you."

They quickly joined him, climbing over the railing and spinning the wooden wheel on the bridge. "How did it ever get here?" Amy asked.

"I had it built. For you and your brother."

"For us?" Tod said, something doubtful in his tone. He was sitting on the railing, his thin legs dangling, looking over every painted inch of the bridge. The old man was concerned. Tod had been out of sorts ever since the previous afternoon when he had found him crying in the woods. Even last night, when Mr. McGregor had burned logs in the fireplace for them and popped corn in a tin pan, the boy had remained aloof, keeping to himself on the big stuffed sofa in the living room. Amy had whispered to him a few times, her face grave like an adult's, but when the old man asked him what was wrong he remained sullen and silent.

"That's right, for you," Mr. McGregor said, hoping to draw him out.

"What's inside?" Tod jumped down from the railing and pounded the closed wooden door.

"Not so hard," the old man scolded.

But the boy kept pounding, and Amy joined him, smashing her tiny fists against the door as if her brother had started a game.

"Stop that," Mr. McGregor said. He removed a key and fitted it into the lock. "Now close your eyes," he told them.

"Why?" Tod asked.

"I want to surprise you."

Tod frowned. "We don't like surprises."

Mr. McGregor sighed and pushed open the door so they could scramble inside. He hung back, watching them stop in the middle of the room and gaze at the marble soda fountain and the little portholes that looked out over an ocean of grass. "Do you like it?" he asked hesitantly.

Instead of answering they wandered about in circles, Amy spinning the seats on the wire stools, Tod poking at the coils of hemp in the corner. The little girl regarded her face in the heart-shaped mirror; she preened and pouted, tying an imaginary ribbon in her hair. Her eyes sought his, gray in the glass, but there was a quality about them, a narrow blankness, that made him uneasy. Perhaps it was because they were Ruthie's eyes. Yes, that must be it.

Tod had found the brass-bound chest. "What's in here?"

"Nothing."

The boy tugged at the padlock with both hands. "Open it."

"Just a pile of old junk," Mr. McGregor explained. He held up a stuffed pirate doll with a rubber knife in its mouth. "Did you see this?"

Tod probed along the edges of the trunk with his fingernails. "Come here," he called to his sister.

The girl was still poised at the mirror, fascinated by her face and hair. She touched the reflected eyes with her thumb.

"Come *here,*" Tod repeated, more insistent. "I want to see what's inside."

The old man moved forward. "I'll open it," he said softly.

110

"It really wouldn't interest you. Just some old books and pictures and things."

"Let's see."

Mr. McGregor bent down. He didn't want to open the chest; he had shut those memories away—his grandchildren's school books, Ruthie's kindergarten drawings on crude brown paper, Mark's third grade projects, a stack of report cards, pictures from the family album. The pictures were the most painful; it had been a long time since he had confronted their photographed faces smiling at him from cribs and highchairs. The little girl had left the mirror, drawn by her curiosity. She stood beside him, studying the chest with bright, puzzled eyes.

They could look if they wished; he didn't have to. He fumbled with the key and then dropped it. Tod retrieved it and unlocked the chest by himself. The old man strode away to one of the portholes, feeling threatened. The trunk and the house held too many mementos. They seemed to lie in wait for him around corridors and in closed rooms, like drifts of unexpected snow. Year by year he had retreated from them, making his world his bedroom, reducing his personal objects to the glass on the night table and the string around his neck.

The hinges creaked, and there was the soft flutter of things being removed. From a corner of his unwilling eye he saw the children spreading the contents on the floor. Go ahead, he thought ruefully, ask me about the photographs.

But they didn't ask. He could hear them rooting in the chest, examining each object in turn. They passed the books and papers from hand to hand in complete silence.

Mr. McGregor suddenly felt spied upon; they were taking advantage of his good nature. "Put those things away," he said abruptly.

The children glanced at him, surprised but not frightened. The little girl was holding one of Ruthie's dolls to her blouse.

111

It looked like a witch with its black button eyes and red wool hair.

"Go on, put them back where you found them."

Tod began gathering them up, but Amy clung to the doll, trying to hide it behind her skirt.

"The doll, too. It doesn't belong to you. Didn't your mother ever teach you not to take other people's things?" He instantly regretted the remark; he had promised himself never to mention their mother.

Amy's arm shot out. She flung the doll over the lid, and it bounced soundlessly in the chest. She placed her hands on her hips and glared at him.

"Now lock it," Mr. McGregor told the boy. Tod seemed almost disinterested as he closed the lid and secured the padlock.

"The key," the old man said. He held out his hand.

Tod dropped it in his palm and then crossed to the soda fountain and sat down on one of the stools. He swung around so that his back was presented to both of them. Amy stood perfectly still, her eyes burning through the almost closed slits.

Mr. McGregor ignored her. "I'm going away for an hour or so," he said. "I want you to stay here. There's a box behind the counter full of toys and jigsaw puzzles."

Tod yawned, but Amy's eyes darted to the toy box.

"Is there anything you'd like me to get you from the store?"

The children didn't answer.

"Then I'm leaving. I'll expect you to be right here when I get back."

Before he left he checked the padlock on the chest.

* * *

He ordered a supply of clothing at a department store in Westwood Village and told the clerk to have it delivered as soon as possible. Then, at a nearby supermarket, he purchased the rest of the items on his list. Juggling the grocery bags, he got back in the car and drove around the block to a newspaper stand on the corner. It was presided over by a blind man who identified coins by their size and feel. "The L.A. *Times*," he called through the window.

The news dealer dipped among the racks and handed him a paper. Mr. McGregor paid him and sat parked by the curb, heedless of the horns behind him. He held up the paper with tingling fingers, his eyes devouring the headlines. But there was no announcement of the children's disappearance. He turned quickly to the second page as the horns grew more demanding. Suddenly, a policeman was crouching at the far window. "Let's move it, Pop. Read your paper at home."

Mr. McGregor pumped his head up and down, nodding wildly. The shock of seeing the officer was only a little less disconcerting than the discovery that he was already acting like a criminal. His first thought had been: How can I get away?

He pulled out, thankful that the man hadn't asked for his license. The police probably had a description of the car by now. He drove down the street, searching for a right-hand turn. In the rearview mirror he could see the officer talking to the news dealer. About him?

Careful to stay well within the speed limit, he approached a small green park on the edge of Beverly Hills. Nurses and Hispanic maids were pushing baby carriages and playing with their charges under the trees. Empty benches welcomed him, but he decided to stay in the car. He parked and went carefully through the paper. There was no mention of the kidnapping, not even in the back pages. Startled, he checked again, but there was only the usual summary of domestic and international news. A new freeway was being considered; there had been no rain in the L.A. basin for eighty-six days; a silent film studio in North Hollywood was being auctioned off piece by piece. He flipped to the front page again, his pale hands blackened with print. Not a mention, not a single mention. Something was wrong.

He crumpled the paper and dropped it outside the car, then he looked across at the little park. Two girls were hopping from bench to bench while a maid knitted in the shade. Suppose he abducted them? There would certainly be an item in the next day's paper—it would make the headlines. Something was decidedly wrong.

He drove slowly toward Santa Monica, muttering questions to himself. Why hadn't Dorothy Hubbard called the police? And if she had, why were they keeping it a secret from the papers?

He abandoned the car on a narrow street near some incomplete construction work. There was no one in sight, and he carefully wiped the steering wheel with his handkerchief, obliterating his fingerprints, and brushed some of Skipper's hairs from the front seat covers. He was reminded again of the policeman at the newspaper stand. Were patrol cars even now cruising the streets, looking for an old man with his morning *Times*?

Grabbing the two large bags of groceries, he locked the car and headed for the nearest bus stop. He shifted the brown-paper bags so they were in front of his face, with only his eyes and forehead uncovered. Even when he boarded the bus and sat down, he kept the bags balanced on his knees and peered out between them. At least they'd never be able to catch him in possession of the car. He must remember to get rid of the incriminating key at the earliest opportunity.

* * *

THE PLAYHOUSE

That evening Mr. McGregor consulted a new cookbook he had bought recommending the proper diets for growing children. He prepared a substantial meal, but in his haste and inexperience he burned the gravy and upset a glass of milk all over the little girl's jumper. The children ate quietly, almost moodily, staring down at the festive place mats and declining offers of second helpings. The old man was annoyed with himself. The meal was a debacle and he wished, fleetingly, that Billy Easter was there to help him. It would all be different when he brought Loretta back. Loretta was an excellent cook.

When the dishes had been washed, he sent the children into the living room and turned out the lights in the rest of the house. He announced that he was leaving for a while and that they should stay up until his return.

"When are we going to get a TV set?" Amy asked.

"Tomorrow."

"In color?"

He sighed. "We'll see."

Tod was sprawled on the rug by the fireplace, his hands clasped behind his head. He said nothing, hardly noticed, as the old man went out and locked the door.

He circled the block in the dim, blue night, around and around. The little bungalow seemed shabbier than usual, its awning faded and peeling, the bike still propped on the steps. No lights burned. Maybe it's a trap, the old man thought. His curiosity would lure him to the door, and then policemen would spring from the shadows with handcuffs. But the more he circled the block, the more convinced he became that the house was empty. The garage door was closed, so he couldn't tell if the convertible was parked inside. Perhaps she was at the bar with her actor friend. It was all very odd.

115

* * *

When he returned to the house he found Amy fast asleep on the sofa, one of her legs thrown over the armrest. Tod was no longer on the floor. "Tod?" he called, moving past the kitchen and down the corridor. Skipper lumbered inquisitively up the steps from the cellar, his nose gray with dust. "Where's your new friend?" the old man asked him. The dog wagged its tail and settled down on its haunches.

Mr. McGregor pondered. He had given firm instructions that they were to remain in the living room until his return. The girl was obedient but Tod, like all boys, was a bit willful and undisciplined. "Tod!" he called again, loudly. "Where are you?"

Then he heard a low sobbing sound. It was almost the same as the day before when he had paused in the little thicket and listened for some clue to the boy's whereabouts.

He hurried up the stairs. It was coming from the children's bedroom, a single sigh like air escaping from a balloon. He knocked on the door. "Tod? Are you all right?"

The crying stopped instantly. "Yes," the boy said, his voice muffled by a blanket or a pillow.

"May I come in?"

"No." The tone was sharp.

"What's wrong? Why have you been crying?"

"Go away."

"I don't want you to be upset. If you're homesick perhaps we can talk."

"Go away." There was a lull of silence and then some hoarse coughing.

"Are you sick?"

"Go away!" the boy screamed at him.

Mr. McGregor backed down the stairs. There had been genuine anger in Tod's voice. Maybe he should consult the little girl; perhaps she knew what was bothering her brother.

Amy was stretching and yawning on the sofa when he entered the living room. Some of the wool from the fabric had stuck to a corner of her sleep-wet mouth, and she was pulling it away like bubble-gum. "Did you bring the set?" she asked in a tired voice.

"I told you I'd get it tomorrow."

"Oh. I thought it was tomorrow already."

The upstairs sobbing had commenced again. Mr. McGregor held a finger to his lips and gestured at the ceiling. "Listen," he whispered.

The little girl shrugged as if the noise was natural, as much a part of the house as Skipper's bark.

"How long has he been crying?" Mr. McGregor asked.

"I don't know. Since you left."

He sat down on the sofa, and she pulled up her legs to give him more room. "Tell me what's wrong with him, Amy."

"Things," the little girl said.

"What kind of things?"

She snuggled against him, her blue school skirt a mass of wrinkles. "I'm hungry," she said. "Do you have any candy?"

"Some chocolates."

She was disappointed. "No M and Ms?"

"No. Tell me about your brother."

"I don't like chocolates as much as I like chocolate milk," she confided. "They get in my teeth and make them sore."

"When was the last time you and Tod went to the dentist?"

"I don't remember." She giggled.

"What's funny?"

"The doctor. He gave me a water pistol to wash out my mouth. It tickled."

Mr. McGregor shifted on the couch. "Tell me why your brother's crying," he asked gently.

"Do you have any crackers with peanut butter?"

He tried to visualize the inside of the refrigerator. Yes—Billy Easter always kept his own private jar of peanut butter somewhere in the back. There were crackers, too, but they were probably stale. "Would you mind stale crackers?"

"I don't think so."

Aware that he was bribing her, the old man went dutifully to the kitchen and hunted for the jar of peanut butter. The crying had subsided, and outside the night was still. He realized that he was very glad the two children were in the house; he was no longer afraid of the sounds in the bushes and the slide of shadows across the lawn.

When he returned to the living room Amy was asleep again, her blonde head pressed into a crack in the cushions, her hands squeezed between her knees. "Amy," he said, touching her shoulder, "wake up, honey."

The eyes blinked open. Blue eyes. Ruthie looking at him. "Make me a cracker," she yawned.

Mr. McGregor scooped out the peanut butter with a kitchen knife.

"Double-deckers," she said. "My mother always makes us double-deckers."

"Don't get crumbs on the sofa," he said lightly, handing her the plate with the crackers. "Tod's stopped crying. Did you notice?"

She nodded, nibbling. "He's a crybaby."

"He must have a reason."

"I guess."

Mr. McGregor searched her face. "You said before you knew why."

"I do. He's sad about our mother."

The old man leaned closer. "Because you can't see her anymore?"

"Uh-uh." The cracker snapped in her mouth. "Because she's dead."

He was shocked, speechless. He could see her calm eyes moving over his face. "Dead?" he repeated. "But—how did it happen?"

"In her sleep," the little girl said. "Could I have another cracker?"

He stared at her, amazed by her casual attitude. "When?"

"Two nights ago. Tod found her before we went to school the next morning. She was lying in bed with her hair in curlers."

Mr. McGregor stood up, breathing heavily. Here she was, delicately eating peanut butter crackers while her brother cried himself to sleep. He was almost repelled by her. "Has anyone *found* her?" he asked, knowing he must go to the boy and comfort him.

"Nobody. We left her there."

Something in her tone was false. Mr. McGregor subjected her to a closer scrutiny. She had her fingers pressed to her mouth and she was trembling all over with an uncontainable excitement—she reminded him of Tod the day on the school lawn when he had known his mother was coming and kept it a secret. "You've been lying to me!" he said.

The child giggled into her fingers. "You're funny."

"Your mother isn't dead. Why did you tell me that?"

She tried to spring away, but Mr. McGregor took her by the arm. "I don't know," she said, her face flushed.

He held her firmly. "Where's your mother? Why isn't she at home?"

Amy seemed exhausted by her laughter. She lay back against the cushions and tried to catch her breath. "She went away."

"Where? And don't lie to me."

"Far away. With Jay."

Mr. McGregor brought her closer. "Look at me, Amy. I want you to tell me the truth. Where did your mother go?"

"With Jay. I *told* you." She brushed a cracker crumb from her lips. "You can ask Tod. She left him a note."

He suddenly remembered the folded scrap of paper in the glade. "What did it say?"

Her shoulders twisted under the white blouse. "I didn't see it. Tod threw it in the fire last night when we were eating popcorn."

Mr. McGregor released her and massaged the little red ring on her wrist. "When is your mother coming back?"

Amy crawled across the sofa and put her arms around him. "She's not. She told Tod we should go to the neighbors."

He found himself growing furious. The woman had literally abandoned them, she had flown away to Puerto Rico with the young man who needed a haircut. It was an unspeakable abdication of responsibility. Did she expect the children to fend for themselves forever? Or was she coming back? She obviously wasn't concerned about the police. If they became involved at all, they'd make perfunctory inquiries, but they'd be no better at finding runaway parents than runaway children. Eventually a social agency would pursue the matter, but that was a long way down the road. He had plenty of time.

He tenderly stroked the little girl's back. She was breathing deeply but she wasn't crying. "Do you want another cracker or some warm milk?"

She shook her head.

He rocked her in his arms, thinking. Dorothy Hubbard had instructed her son to go to the neighbors, but he had disobeyed her. Instead, dazed and dispirited, he continued his normal routine, going to school and taking his sister along with him. And Mr. McGregor had picked them up like two stray kittens. No wonder Tod had cried and hardly touched his food.

"Do you miss her?" he asked softly.

She reflected, then she said in an even voice, "I hate her."

"And Tod? Does he hate her, too?"

"I haven't asked him."

"What about your father?"

"I don't remember him. He ran away."

He looked into her hair, and it was light and fine like his granddaughter's. Loretta had combed it every night before the fireplace. Ruthie in her cotton pajamas, sucking on a peppermint stick. He tightened his arms around Amy. "You won't have to worry anymore," he said.

The little girl lifted her face. "Can we stay here?"

"Of course. You and Tod can stay as long as you like."

She threw her arms around him.

It couldn't have been more perfect, the old man thought with considerable satisfaction. The sisters would grow concerned over the children's continued absence from school and call or go to the house. The neighbors would inform them that Mrs. Hubbard had gone away; she had obviously taken her son and daughter with her. End of inquiry. They were both his.

He picked up the little girl and set her on the floor. "Time for bed," he said. "You're falling asleep again."

Amy nodded, rubbing her eyes and pushing the tangled hair from her face. "I like you," she said.

Mr. McGregor smiled. "I like you too."

Amy moved sluggishly to the stairway, then turned back. "Remember tomorrow," she said. "The TV set."

He almost had to laugh. "I won't forget. Do you want me to tuck you in?"

"No, I can go to bed by myself."

The old man listened as she padded up the stairs. She had squashed a peanut butter cracker on the sofa, but he didn't care. The children were his. Everything had managed to unravel and work itself out. They had had an unfortunate

life—no father and a young girl masquerading as a mother—
but they wouldn't have to worry again. He'd see to it.

He was pouring himself a brandy nightcap when he felt
a draft on his legs. It seemed to be running through the
corridor from the direction of the kitchen. Skipper slept
soundly, undisturbed by the new cool current.

Mr. McGregor entered the kitchen. The window over the
sink was wide open, the panes gleaming with moonlight.
The faucet dripped noisily.

He stared at the window, trying to recall if he had opened
it. No—he remembered checking the catch late in the afternoon. It couldn't have come open by itself, unless Amy or
the boy had felt stuffy in the living room and wanted some
air. Confused, he closed the window and groped his way
upstairs to bed, reminding himself to ask them in the morning.

The luminous alarm clock looked at him, a frowning face.
He had come out of a restless sleep, his head hot, his eyes
twitching at the corners. Eleven o'clock. He had slept for
only an hour. The open window still bothered him, it was
a crack in his careful fortifications. Even here in the bedroom he imagined he could feel the draft coiling its way
upstairs and tying an icy string of air around his ankle. But
that was impossible—the window was closed.

He rolled groggily out of bed and pulled on his nightgown. His feet slapped on the cold wooden floor, reviving
him, and he stuffed them into his slippers. He took his
flashlight from the night table drawer and left his room,
moving down the corridor to where the children slept in the
other wing.

They were safe under the covers, the patchwork blanket
hiding them as if they were buried under layers of leaves.

Tod was talking in his sleep, and the old man moved closer, but the words were meaningless.

As he started back to his room he heard something fall in the kitchen. He froze, his ears straining, then he began to tiptoe down the steps, holding up the over-long skirts of his nightgown. Perhaps it was Skipper blundering around his water bowl or teasing the kittens.

He reached the kitchen and went to the window. It was closed, just as he had left it. Then he turned quickly, on an impulse. A heavy glass tumbler was lying on the linoleum floor. He brought his eyes up slowly and saw a bottle of rum standing on the kitchen table, shining with light like a huge inverted thimble. Seated at the table, one languid leg hooked over the edge, was Billy Easter. "Hey, Mr. Mc-Gregor," he said, his teeth flashing a friendly smile. He was petting one of the kittens.

Astonished, the old man drew back.

The black man grinned and reached down, picking up the water tumbler. He poured a large amount of rum into the glass and drank it. He was wearing a checkered shirt, open at the throat, with the sleeves rolled tightly to the armpits. He seemed perfectly relaxed except for the restlessly dangling leg.

"What are you doing here?" the old man sputtered. He was too startled to even turn on the light.

"I got worried about you, Mr. McGregor, puttering around here all by yourself. You were never much of a cook—I see you burned that pan in the sink."

"How did you get in?"

Billy gestured toward the window. "That catch couldn't keep out a bumblebee. You just better get yourself a whole new set of locks."

"Damn the window," the old man said. "How did you get in the gate?"

Billy crooked a sly finger to his lips. "That's a secret."

"You'll tell me!" he said, his voice cracking. "You'll tell me, or I'll call the police!"

"Hey, now. You keep shouting, and you're gonna wake your two little friends upstairs."

Mr. McGregor narrowed his eyes and drew the string on his nightgown tighter. "How did you know about them?" he asked.

Billy chuckled and poured more rum. "Sure you don't want some of this apple juice?"

"I asked you how you knew about the children."

"That's simple. I been following you."

The old man jerked up, aghast. "Following me?"

"Uh-huh. You picked 'em up at that school. I saw the whole thing."

"You've been spying again!"

Billy finished another glass. "Guess I have at that. I mean, hell, you were sure up to something. And I wasn't about to swallow that one-legged story about you moving away to an apartment house."

The old man felt shaky, as if he had been turned upside down. He shook his head to clear it.

Billy moved to his side. "You don't look so good," he said. He pulled over one of the kitchen chairs. "Better take the weight off."

Mr. McGregor sank into the chair. It all seemed so unreal; the last few days had never happened. It was almost as if he had spent half his life with Billy Easter at this table while the cats slept by the stove and the old house creaked. Were the children still upstairs? Or was the bed just covered with the little hills of empty blankets?

"Cheer up," Billy said brightly. "So I know about the kids. So what?"

Somehow Mr. McGregor didn't feel comforted. Billy's smiling face was close to his, and he had the uneasy feeling that their roles had been reversed. "What do you want?" he asked.

"Nothing much. Just the same as always. I mean, with two kids around you need somebody to do the cooking and drive the car. Am I right?"

The old man just stared at him.

"Course, with all this extra work I figure I should get a raise. You know? Like maybe three-hundred a week." He hesitated, waiting for a reaction.

Mr. McGregor sighed heavily. Three-hundred, four-hundred—what did it really matter? He was tired of fighting with the man. You put him out in yesterday's trash, and there he was, sitting on your doorstep in the morning. What was that toy he had once bought Mark? A boomerang?

"We got a deal?" Billy asked, then he added, before the old man could voice a mild protest, "And don't go talking about the cops. You snatched those kids. That's called kidnapping around here."

"They were abandoned by their mother," Mr. McGregor said softly.

"Sure," said Billy, "if you say so. But that's not the point. Do you want me to call the cops or don't you?"

"Don't call them."

Billy smiled and regarded the old man with affection. "You're one of a kind, you know that? First I thought you was after that blonde. But it was the kids all the time, wasn't it?"

"I'm going to bed," Mr. McGregor announced. He had no intention of discussing it further. The exorbitant salary would have to cover the gaps in Billy's knowledge.

"You want me up at any special time tomorrow?"

"No."

Billy tugged his suitcase from beneath the table. "See? I came back with everything. My bedroom still the same?"

"The same."

Billy watched him for a long moment. "How long you figuring on keeping those kids here?"

"Just stay away from them," the old man said, letting the chauffeur see the full force of his tired anger. "Let them be. I don't want you near them."

Billy bowed his head, suppressing a grin. "Anything you say, Mr. McGregor."

The old man left without a word and hobbled slowly up the stairs.

Billy Easter stood in his bare feet on the driveway, hosing down the car. Then he scooped up two foaming sponges and scraped away at the heavy, caked dirt and the little white stars of bird droppings. Why am I breaking my butt? he thought.

He had been at the house for almost two days, and he had never worked harder in his life. Scrubbing down walls in the deserted wing, defrosting the refrigerator, moving more toys into the playhouse, cooking three solid meals a day—his muscles ached, and there was a corn forming on the ball of his right foot. He even had to drive into the Village to pick up a new television set.

The set really irritated him. He had been after the old man for a year to buy one, but the answer had always been no. Now the kids move in and presto!—there was a big fat RCA. He had spent the night on his hands and knees laying a cord and connecting it to the outside antenna. And all because of the kids.

He leaned an elbow on the hood and let some of the sponge water sluice down the back of his neck. Two days on the job, and he had hardly seen the children. He'd cook their breakfast in the morning, and then McGregor would make him go outside to weed the lawn. After lunch they'd vanish, exploring the estate or going to the playhouse, and in the evenings they'd watch TV until nine. He was allowed to use the set until midnight, but by that time he was heading out through the tunnel to see his old lady.

Something sharp poked him in the back. He spun around warily and saw the boy ducking behind the side of the car. "Hey you!" he said. "What's the big idea?"

The boy strolled out casually from his concealment. His sister was with him, carrying a jar that was full of bugs.

"Don't you go sticking people in the back with that thing."

The boy had a long, twisted branch he had obviously snapped loose from one of the trees. He inspected Billy for a full ten seconds before he pointed the stick again and tapped him on the foot.

"What did I just say?" Billy was impressed in spite of himself by the child's courage. "You want me to go tell Mr. McGregor? He'll put a yard of red welts across your bottom."

"Who are you?" asked the little girl.

"Who am *I*?" Billy was forced to grin. "Who do you think cooks your food? Who lugged that damn TV set into the house?"

"What's your name?" the boy asked solemnly. The stick dug in the dirt around the chauffeur's foot, tracing it.

"Billy. What's yours?"

The boy didn't answer but the little girl said, "Amy. Do you live here?"

"If you can call it living. What've you two been up to?"

The boy tapped his foot again with the stick.

Billy put down the sponge. "Now listen, you. If you don't cut that out I'm gonna break you *and* that stick in half."

The boy leaned on his weapon and rapidly blinked his eyes.

"What's that supposed to mean? You got something in your eye?"

"Where do you sleep?" the little girl asked.

"In a bed."

She giggled and offered him the glass jar. "Do you know what's in here?"

"Nuts and bolts?" he kidded her.

"No, they're not. They're beetles. Have you ever seen a newt?"

"A what?"

"A newt."

He laughed and began working on the car again. "That's one on me. Don't you kids go to school anymore?"

"We don't have to," the little girl said. "Haven't you *ever* seen a newt?"

"Not if I can help it." He glanced at the boy who was leaning on the stick, watching him. "What's your brother's name?"

"Tod," the boy answered.

"Hey, you talk, huh? I thought maybe you didn't have no tongue. You're pretty lucky not to have to go to school anymore."

"It's boring."

"School?"

The stick was tossed across the drive. "Around here," he said. "Who are those kids?"

Billy Easter turned, scanning the lawn. "What kids? I don't see no kids."

"The ones he has pictures of."

"Pictures?"

"He keeps them in that chest in the playhouse." The boy's lashes flickered for an instant.

"You been in there?" Billy asked.

"He says he'll let us play in the cabin if we don't go near the chest."

128

Billy turned back to the car, and he could see the child's inquisitive face reflected on the hood. He didn't like the face so he placed a wet sponge in its center.

"Well?" Tod said. "Who are the kids?"

"His grandchildren."

"How come they're never around?"

"Billy!" The voice seemed to drop straight down from the sky. The chauffeur swung around and looked up. Mr. McGregor was standing at a window on the second floor. "Get to work on that car," he called. "Didn't I tell you to leave the children alone?"

"Yes, sir," Billy said. "But maybe you ought to tell them to leave *me* alone."

The boy spoke without moving his lips. It was like a ventriloquist's dummy Billy had once seen on television. "How come they're never here?" he whispered.

Billy didn't answer. He walked to the edge of the gravel drive to get a tin of car wax.

"Tod! Amy!" the old man called. "Come into the house."

Billy watched them. They didn't respond immediately. In fact, they seemed to be asserting themselves, taking their own sweet time. Their heads were raised, looking up, as if the old man was some papier-mâché face on the end of a stick, hovering in the window. Then the boy took his sister's hand, and they went slowly toward the house, the little girl still clutching her jar.

Billy rubbed some wax on a rag and began coating the hood. He wondered if he should have mentioned the grandchildren, but he decided it didn't matter. Why the hell had he come back? The old man was a constant thorn in his side and now, with the two kids, it was somehow worse. Especially the little boy.

Just take your money, he thought. In a few short weeks he'd be heading South, flying like a bird. He pretended he was already there, feeling the warm Caribbean sun.

* * *

Mr. McGregor sat watching the late news. The children and Billy were long in bed. Logs burned in the fireplace, sending wavering shadows over the television screen. The knowledge that he was perfectly safe gave him a rare feeling of repose. Even Billy's unexpected reappearance was more a comfort than a hindrance; it relieved him of domestic chores and permitted him to enjoy the children. There was no mention of their disappearance on the local news, and now the anchor people were finishing up with sports and weather.

Mr. McGregor settled back on the sofa, lighting his last cigar of the day. He'd give Tod and Amy another week to acclimate themselves to the new environment. There was progress already. They seemed to be thriving on Billy's cooking, and they had accepted the routine of the household without a qualm. He felt guilty because of their neglected school work, but he planned to buy some educational books that they could read and study at home. Loretta would be helpful in that area; she had been an elementary school teacher before she married Norman, and he was sure she would develop some kind of tutoring schedule for the children. He could envision her face when he brought her back from the sanitarium—surprised, then radiant. The expectation warmed him.

The late news ended, and Amy came into the room and crawled up on his lap. "What a nice surprise," he said. "But you should really be in bed."

"What are you watching?" she asked. She was wearing a set of pajamas that had been delivered with the other clothes. They were similar to the kind Ruthie once wore, bright blue with the white faces of rabbits on the back and front. Her blonde hair was brushed, and he could detect the sweet odor of toothpaste on her breath.

"The late show," he said. "Is Tod asleep?"

"Uh-huh. He didn't say his prayers tonight."

The old man squashed out his cigar. "We'll have to get after him about that. Is he feeling any better now?"

"Okay, I guess." She reached up and touched his ear. "Why do you have such big ears?"

"I don't know," he laughed. "My father had big ears."

"Will he come to the house?"

"No, I'm afraid not. He isn't here anymore. He lived in Michigan all his life."

She tugged his other ear. "Where's Michigan?"

"Far away. It's very cold, and it snows all the time."

"I never saw snow."

"It's very nice. Cold, and pretty, and it tastes like ice-cream."

"Does Santa Claus live in Michigan?"

"No, he's farther north."

She rested her head against his chest, her eyes on the television screen. The yellow firelight turned her long blonde hair to straw. "Do you know something?" she said. "I have a secret."

"Is it a nice secret?"

She stood up on the sofa and cupped her hands to his ear. "Want to know what it is?" she whispered.

"Naturally."

"My birthday's tomorrow."

"Your birthday!" he said. "Why didn't you tell me sooner?"

"I just remembered it." She blushed. "Tod told me."

"Well!" said Mr. McGregor, bouncing her in his lap. "Isn't that something. We'll have to have a party."

"Could we?"

"Of course. A birthday cake and ice cream and maybe—"

"Maybe what?"

"Maybe—if you're a good girl and you take those vitamins I bought you—maybe there might be some presents, too."

"Do you think," she began in a grave voice, "do you think I might get some newts?"

"Fish?"

"A friend of mine in school had a whole bowl of them, but they died."

"I'm sorry to hear that. Yes, I guess we could get you some newts."

The little girl wiggled her fingers. "They swim funny. And they're mostly pink with little spots on them."

"They sound like chicken pox," he smiled.

She looked at him crossly. "No, they're not. They're *animals*."

"I know, Amy. I'm just teasing."

"Can I invite some of my friends to the party?"

He shook his head and lifted her to the floor. "Not this year. This is going to be our own private party—just you, and Tod, and me."

"Will Billy come?"

"I don't know. We'll see."

She suddenly put her two warm hands to his cheeks and kissed him. "Goodnight."

"Nighty-night, dear." He watched her, glowing, as she crossed the carpet and ran nimbly up the steps. He was settling back on the sofa again when he heard the tiny hiss of whispers somewhere above on the landing.

Not making a sound, he moved carefully to the archway and looked up. Two small shadows, heads almost touching, were conferring at the top of the stairs. The light was dim, but he could make out part of Tod's new plaid robe. The whispering continued, then the shadows marched down the hallway, the taller leading the shorter.

132

Still listening, Mr. McGregor heard the door to the bedroom close. He had a suspicion that the boy had been standing there during his conversation with Amy, that he had sent his sister down in the first place. Why had she told him Tod was asleep?

Mr. McGregor went back to the sofa. He sat down, welcoming the wavering fire on his face. Newts, he thought. Where could he buy some newts?

The playhouse blazed like a bonfire. All the copper ship's lanterns were lit, and they were strung out merrily along the bridge like bright bobbing apples.

The old man came from the house with the children. They had just finished dinner, and Billy Easter had slipped secretly away from the kitchen to prepare the playhouse for the festivities. Mr. McGregor was overwhelmed. The ship looked so authentic in the twilight that he wanted to weigh anchor, start the motors, and go sailing down Sunset Boulevard.

"It's beau-ti-ful," Amy gasped

"What do you think, Tod?" Mr. McGregor asked.

"Not bad."

"Then come aboard, mates," he boomed out, sweeping his arm toward the entrance.

The children clamored up the steps and into the cabin. Mr. McGregor followed them, pausing to polish one of the copper lanterns with his jacket sleeve.

Inside the cabin was semi-dark, shadowed, with the lingering traces of warm twilight at the portholes. A table was set in the center of the room with a white linen cloth and two lit candles in silver holders. In the middle of the table was a large angel food cake with *"Happy Birthday, Amy"* spelled out in sugary letters on its shining surface. Billy Easter stood nearby holding a giant box of matches and an ice cream scoop.

Mr. McGregor drew back a chair for Amy, and the children sat down, the candlelight dancing on their new clothes and clean fingernails. The old man pulled up another chair for himself and nodded imperceptibly to Billy.

The chauffeur struck a long match and lit each of the candles on the cake. "Whew!" Amy breathed, drawing away from the heat of the fire on her face. The black man stepped back, his arms folded.

"Now," said Mr. McGregor, "all together. . . ." He raised his arms, holding an invisible baton. "Happy birthday to you . . ." he sang, beckoning for the children to join in.

They began tentatively, Tod singing in a shy boy's voice, Amy like a squeaky mouse. Billy Easter was silent, sneaking a glance at his watch.

When the song was over Mr. McGregor sliced three wedges from the cake. "Ice cream," he called while he passed out the plates. Billy removed a quart container from the little icebox built into the soda fountain, scooping out portions and dropping them on the individual pieces of cake. "Thank you, Billy," the old man said. "You're excused."

Billy tossed the scoop on the marble counter and went out without a word.

As the children ate their cake, Mr. McGregor crossed to a dark corner of the cabin and returned with a pile of gifts wrapped in silver paper. He had spent most of the afternoon prowling toy stores and pet shops, and he held his breath as Amy shoved aside her food with a hoot of pleasure and attacked the first present. The boy sat quietly, the spoon with a massive chunk of cake held arrested near his mouth.

"It's a doll!" the little girl cried. "But it's *old*." She stared at it, confused, her eyes appealing to the old man.

"It belonged to my granddaughter," he said. "Remember?

You were looking at it the other day, and I got angry with you. I want you to have it."

She covered it with the silver strips of paper. "I don't like it anymore," she said, turning her attention to the second package. The old man closed his eyes for a moment. When he opened them Amy was frowning again, her face wrinkled like an old woman's. "School books?" she muttered in disbelief.

"We're going to have lessons to do," the old man said. "We mustn't forget your education." He knew there was no way to sweeten the fact.

"No," the little girl said emphatically. "No lessons." She hid the books under the wrappings. One present remained, an oddly shaped package tied with a yellow bow. Amy regarded it scornfully. What was lurking behind the gay paper and ribbons? Castor oil, a trip to the dentist? "*You* open it," she said to Tod.

The boy shook his head. It seemed to Mr. McGregor that there was an amused glint in his eye. Prepared for anything, Amy slowly tore the paper away. For a few seconds she was confused again; there was something made of glass inside with a rubber membrane stretched across the top. But when she stripped off the rest of the wrapping her face glowed with delight. Two tiny creatures were swimming about, pinkish and spotted under the low lights of the lanterns and the candles. "Newts!" she exclaimed. "My newts!"

Mr. McGregor smiled. He had known that the last gift was surefire, something to take the sting from the books.

Amy tapped her fingers on the side of the bowl. "They're beautiful," she cried, holding it up to the candles. Even Tod seemed interested. He tinkled his spoon against the bowl. "You'll frighten them," she cautioned.

He shrugged. "They're only salamanders."

"They're *not*. Salamanders are different. These are newts." She appealed to Mr. McGregor. "Aren't they?"

135

"I really don't know," he admitted. "But the man in the pet shop told me to be sure to remove the rubber cover. They have to breathe. But he said they also have a way of climbing out of the bowl if you don't watch out."

"We'll get a piece of cardboard, and we'll punch some holes in it," Amy said.

"Fine." The old man removed a box from his pocket. "Here's what they eat. When you run out of this let me know, and I'll order some more."

The girl read the lettering on the box. Her brother swung out of the chair, dropping his napkin on the floor.

"Better pick it up," the old man said.

Tod hesitated, then tossed off an elaborate shrug, bent down and speared it. He suddenly caught it around his sister's eyes as she peered into the depths of the bowl.

"Stop that!" she howled, snatching it away.

"What's wrong?" Mr. McGregor asked him. "You were acting like a little gentleman there for a while."

"I'm tired of this party," Tod said, spinning in a circle.

"Careful," the old man warned, "you'll get dizzy."

Tod allowed himself to fall forward, his hands shooting out at the last moment to break his fall. "Let's do something else."

The old man realized that he had been catering to Amy for the past few days, making her the center of attention. It was only natural that the boy would rebel; he deserved some indulgence. "All right, what would you like to do? Any ideas?"

Tod sat down in his chair, his legs wrapping around the rungs. "Why don't you tell us a story?"

"I'm afraid I'm not very good with stories. I don't think I really know any."

"Sure you do," Amy said, drawing her chair closer. "Everybody knows at least one story."

136

Tod was looking across the room. "Tell us about what's in that sea chest. The pictures and stuff."

The old man lay down his fork. They wanted a story. Hansel and Gretel, the prince who turned into a frog? No, those would be considered old-fashioned by children who had grown up with television's hall of mirrors. Besides, he could hardly recall them any longer; it had been years since he sat on Ruthie's bed with the big illustrated copy of Grimm's in his lap. What was the one she loved the most? The King and the White Snake. How did it go? Something about a snake under a silver chafing dish that was delivered to the monarch's chamber every evening before he went to bed. He couldn't remember the rest of it.

Preoccupied, knowing the children were waiting, he walked to the porthole over the sea chest. He would have to make one up. But where would he start? "Once," he began, experimentally, "once upon a time there was a king. He lived in a big castle surrounded for miles and miles by woods. . . ."

"Was he rich?" Amy asked.

"Very rich. He had dozens of chariots and six stables of black horses. He lived with his family—the queen, and his daughter, and her husband the prince, and his two little heirs."

"What are heirs?" the girl asked.

"Children," Mr. McGregor explained. Suddenly he looked down at the sea chest. What was he telling them?

"Go on." Amy fidgeted in the chair.

"Well . . . the king loved his children. He loved them more than all his horses and his chariots and all the people in his castle."

"Did they love him?"

"Oh, yes. Every night he would read to them and tell them stories. Sometimes he even forgot his other duties because he was so happy with his children." Stop here, he told himself. What could he hope to achieve by continuing?

"And then?" the little girl prompted him. Tod was pinching at the tablecloth, bored, lifting it up to form miniature pyramids among the plates.

"And then . . ." and then what? "And then one afternoon the king's children wanted to go to the village and visit a magic toy shop. And . . . and the king decided he would take them himself."

Amy frowned. "But why couldn't the king just make some toys appear in their room?"

"Because this king—he was just an ordinary king, he had no special powers. So he had his servant bring his finest chariot to the door. And he put his children in the back seat, and he drove the black horses himself. Only—" He swallowed, bewildered. It was forcing itself out as if someone was dictating to him. He spoke compulsively, without control.

"Only?" Amy prodded.

"Only—only the king was careless, terribly careless. He drove the horses too fast. And when the chariot went around a corner its wheel hit a tree, and the chariot—the whole chariot with the king and his children—it turned upside down in the road. All the way up in the air and then upside down in the road." Don't ask anymore. Please don't ask anymore.

"What happened to the king? Did he die?"

The old man shook his head slowly from side to side.

"What about the children?"

He didn't answer.

"Did the children die?"

He bent over the chest and traced his hand along the smooth brass bands. All the king's horses and all the king's men, couldn't put. . . .

Amy jumped out of the chair, breaking the mood. "I

don't like your story," she said. "Let's go for a walk."

Tod wrinkled his nose. "We haven't played any games," he said. "Let's play a game."

"Which one?" Amy asked.

"Hide and seek." He glanced at the old man for approval.

Mr. McGregor was still running his hand along the chest. He felt himself trembling. He should have told them Hansel and Gretel. But something had possessed him, some clumsy, perverse desire to share the truth with them, even if it had to be disguised as a fable. Yet, when he brought himself to look at them, he saw that it didn't matter; they had already forgotten the story and were expectantly awaiting his decision. "It's getting late," he said, pulling himself together. "Don't you think—"

"No!" Amy said, tugging at his arm. "It's not bedtime yet. Just one little game. Okay?"

Tod tagged him on the back. "You're it!" he cried. "Close your eyes and count to a hundred."

The little boy's words, half-remembered, touched Mr. McGregor with a sharp sense of nostalgia. *Tag, you're it.* He had a sudden recollection of his youth and all the hide-and-seek games tumbling together into one particular morning when he had concealed himself in a hayloft, close to a drift of straw, and huddled there for over an hour while his friends searched fruitlessly below. He could spy on them through a timbered archway, and at that moment he had such a feeling of power that he shook with excitement. There he was, high and safe, observing but unobserved, an all-seeing eye. And now Tod and Amy desired that same secret pleasure. Well, why shouldn't they have their fun? By telling his fairy tale he had tried to involve them in his own dark broodings; this was a way to make amends. There were probably very few games of any sort when they lived with their mother.

He lowered his head to his arm on the table, trying to

recapture the mood of his day in the hayloft. "One, two, three—" he called out loudly. There was a frenzy of movement, excited whispers, the wooden floor shaking with running feet. "Fourteen . . . fifteen . . . sixteen . . ."

He counted the rest of the numbers in his mind. They obviously couldn't hide in the playhouse, and it occurred to him that they planned to use the whole estate. The idea disturbed him. There were too many places to fall and twist an ankle in the dark. Ninety-nine . . . one hundred. And then, of course, the usual protocol in games of this sort: "Here I come, ready or not!" he shouted.

The cabin was empty. It seemed darker than before, the lanterns throwing a dull, dreamy light. He seemed far out on a lake, water lapping at the side, the boat gliding rudderless.

He rose stiffly from the chair, sadly acknowledging the fact that he was too old for children's games. Bed was more his habitat, a snow-white sea of sheets and peace. Foolish, he thought, moving to the door. He should have tempted them with nightcaps of hot chocolate. Well, he'd find them quickly and send them off to bed.

He went out to the bridge and inspected the house. A point of light burned in Billy's room, the rest of it was dark. He doubted if they had gone inside; the bushes and weeds would be their province. What was the old trick? Decide where you would hide yourself and look for your quarry there.

He left the playhouse and went toward the ragged barrier of grass behind the house, stopping at the line of wild vegetation to sniff the air. Dry, everything was dry. He would have to get Billy out here with his hose. At his feet insects were humming, fiddling deep in the grass. He imagined there was a giant brown grasshopper somewhere in the heart of the trees, scratching and clicking its many legs.

He shouted their names and plunged on. In some spots

the grass was only ankle-high, but in others it reached to his knees. Why hadn't he contacted men with power mowers who could have cut it and carted it away? Then he'd have something to be proud of, emerald lawns as closely cropped as a golf course.

He swept through the shrubbery, no longer calling for them. Finally, when he emerged from a clump of trees, he realized that his mental compass was disrupted. He had been walking in circles, trying to keep the house at his back. Now, in the heavy darkness, he had lost his way. He thought of the children with a growing sense of alarm. Suppose they had separated and wandered off near the boundaries of the estate? Uncharted territory. The boy could take care of himself, but Amy, lost, could remain on the grounds all night while he searched frantically for her.

"Amy!" he called, striking out at the tall stalks of grass around him. His voice seemed small. "It's time to come in. The game's over." There was no wind and nothing stirred in the underbrush. "Tod! Find your sister and go back to the house!"

He rested, leaning against a tree. The moon was behind a cloud, and he seemed in total darkness. It was growing chilly, and he buttoned his jacket, warming his hands in his pockets where he could feel old bits of tobacco and candy crumbs. Were they playing a trick on him? Hiding close by, stifling giggles, while he charged through the grass in desperation? Or had they decided to run away?

This second thought brought him up short. Perhaps their easy acceptance of him and the house was only a pretense. The birthday party and the game had been lures to keep him occupied while they plotted an escape over the fence. Could they climb it? Of course not. But impossible though it was, he still had an unsettling vision of them running down St. Cloud Road in their party clothes.

He moved around the side of the tree and came face to

face with Amy. She was huddled at the base of the trunk, her little arms hugging her body, and she was smiling at him.

Billy Easter could see the playhouse from his bedroom window. It was still lit up like a Christmas tree, and he imagined they were finishing their cake while the old man told stories. A party for two kidnapped kids! He shook his head.

He had changed into Levi's and a torn shirt—his "combat suit" as he liked to think of it. He had ruined enough good clothing on his way through his tunnel every night. If he had any sense at all he'd go down to McGregor and demand the key to the gate. But that, he knew, was only begging for trouble. You were never sure how that crazy old man would react, even if you were holding all the cards. You took the chance he might have a heart attack or grab a knife from the kitchen drawer. No, it was best to hide things from him and keep him guessing.

He closed the door silently behind him and descended to the first floor. The old man might've come back to the kitchen for more ice cream, so he decided to use the front door instead of the back.

As he passed the archway leading to the living room, something caught his eye. He shrank quietly into the hallway shadows, listening. Someone was standing at the built-in bar, rattling among the bottles. McGregor? He moved back, almost stepping on Skipper who was sleeping on the floor. Dog, dog! he thought. One of these days you're gonna be minus a tail.

He peered through the arch. It was the boy, Tod, bent over like a burglar and rummaging around in the old man's liquor supply. How do you like that? Billy mused, holding down a chuckle. A taste for the hard stuff. That boy couldn't

142

be more than ten years old. He crossed past the archway and tiptoed to the front door. If the kid liked to drink, well, that was his problem. Maybe the little girl liked the stuff, too. Give them both a milk bottle full of booze with a nipple on the end, then sit back and watch the fireworks.

He closed the door. It made a sound as the lock snapped home. He crept past the living room window and a small face looked out into the garden. It was Tod, and the boy had seen him.

Damn! Billy thought, jogging now across the front lawn. Why did the kid have to go to the window at just that moment?

He reached the trees and scurried about, searching for his hidden path. It was a cloudy night, the moon popping up now and then like the face of a flashlight. Stay inside, moon. Don't go wandering around where you're not wanted, Billy thought.

He found the path and followed its curving course. This was the worst part: leaving the estate and coming back. If he had any guts he'd kick the old man out of the house and move in with his family. There was enough liquor for a week of parties—providing the kid didn't drink it all up.

Something crackled on the path behind him. Billy whirled just in time to see a small shadow glide behind a tree. Following me, he thought, starting to run again. Wants to know where I'm going. He could hear the light scamper of footfalls behind him. Why didn't he stay in the damn house with the whisky?

The moon had emerged again, flooding the field with a cold, white light. Billy glanced over his shoulder. The shadow was still there, cleaving the wild grass. The hell with it, he thought. If he wants to tell the old man, I'll just let him know what I saw in the living room. Two can play that game.

There was the fence, at last. He dropped to his stomach and began burrowing through the shallow tunnel, worming his way out to the road. Then he stood up and loped across the asphalt toward a zone of palms. Concealing himself, he waited, but the boy seemed to have disappeared. Maybe he had tired of the hunt and retraced his steps. Or maybe he was thirsty again.

He was about to leave when he saw a small figure work its way out from the tunnel and stand panting on the road. It was Tod, his clothing surprisingly unruffled, his hair beautifully combed, the part showing white in the moonlight.

So that was it, Billy thought. Sure. He wants to escape, go back where he came from. But why the hell didn't he bring his sister? Was he going to leave her with that crazy old man?

The boy looked in both directions. There was the hum of a car climbing up the hill from Sunset. He'll thumb a ride, Billy thought. But as the car approached, bearing down on them and whizzing past, Tod made no effort to hail it. Instead, he crouched back into the foliage so that the headlights wouldn't reveal him.

What's his problem? Billy wondered. Why doesn't he take off down the road? The old man was probably still in the playhouse, occupied with the little girl. He was free as a bird, yet there he stood breathing the night air, motionless.

Billy watched him. Why don't you run, boy? he thought. You wanna grow up behind those gates, spend the rest of your life with that crazy old man? What's wrong with you, boy?

Tod turned slowly and then ducked down into the tunnel. He rose on the other side, behind the fence, and began running back toward the house. Billy came out from the row of trees. He was amazed. Even Skipper wouldn't have

144

returned. Show that dog the outside world, and you wouldn't see him again for dust.

He started down the long hill, wondering if he should tell McGregor. No, let him find out for himself. He had taken the two kids, and they were his problem. Billy Easter was going to stay out of it. Just a few more weeks, and he'd have enough money to fly the coop. Just a few more weeks.

The next afternoon Mr. McGregor descended to the cellar and began collecting the things he wanted burned. The objects of importance, the photographs, the special toys, the most personal souvenirs, were safely in the playhouse chest. But there was still a residue that waited in ambush for him in the dim dusty light from the windows—a headless rocking horse, a set of electric trains sprawled like an accident among some old Christmas decorations. These things could be disposed of without betraying memories.

He browsed dreamily, and when he glanced up he saw that Tod had followed him downstairs. The boy was strolling along the lanes of bric-a-brac. "Want to give me a hand?" he asked.

"Not particularly." Tod picked up an old umbrella of Loretta's with a cat's head for a handle. "It's my birthday tomorrow," he announced.

"Your birthday?"

"Yeah. I want a party like Amy had."

"Now don't fib to me," the old man said. "It's not your birthday."

The boy opened the umbrella in a shower of dust. "How do you know it isn't?"

"Close that," Mr. McGregor said.

"Why?"

"It's bad luck opening an umbrella indoors."

The boy made no effort to close it. "I'll give you a list of what I want for presents."

"There won't be a party. If you want anything special tell me, and I'll pick it up the next time I'm in the Village."

The boy twirled the umbrella in his fingers, watching the blur of its ribs. "I want a party," he repeated. "Everything my sister had."

"When it's your real birthday, you'll have a party and not before."

The boy went to the steps. "How do you know it was Amy's real birthday?"

"Because she told me. And I believed her."

Tod smiled. "Maybe I got her to say it was." He went skipping up the steps, balancing the umbrella as if he was on a circus tightrope.

Now what was all *that* about? the old man thought peevishly. He sat down in a broken rocking chair. It was apparent that Tod was jealous of his sister's party—Mark had often made similar you-gave-it-to-her-now-give-it-to-me demands. But why the remark about telling Amy to lie to him? Was it merely another prank? He had scolded them about the hide-and-seek game, but the girl had only laughed and Tod had listened to the dressing down with vast indifference. He rocked back and forth, the chair's round legs clacking on the concrete floor. It would be different with Loretta in the house again. The children needed discipline, a gentle sense of firmness, and she would provide it.

Rising, he went back to work, gathering up the things he wanted destroyed. Today was Tuesday. On Friday he would go out to the sanitarium.

* * *

The sun was sinking, and the earth was a pale, swimming red. Someone on one of the neighboring estates was burning leaves, and a sweet haze drifted across the treetops. Billy Easter left the house purposefully. In a few minutes McGregor would be hounding him to prepare dinner, but there was something he had to attend to first.

There they were—a line of orange crates and cardboard cartons arranged haphazardly in front of a huge old oak. He had seen the boy dragging them out to the woods almost an hour ago. The girl was off somewhere, chasing butterflies on the other side of the estate. But he wasn't interested in her.

"Where are they?" he asked, climbing over one of the crates and confronting Tod. The boy was sitting behind the wall of boxes, dawdling in the dirt with a butter-knife he had taken from the kitchen. Again, even sprawled on the ground, he looked immaculate, a fact that never ceased to rub Billy the wrong way. "Well?" he said. "Hand them over."

Tod barely looked at him. Beside him was a magpie collection of things he had brought from the house: Coke bottles, a tablecloth, an old cigar box, a teak elephant that had stood on the shelf in the living room. "Don't know what you mean," he said, cleaning the knife with the table-cloth.

"You took those car keys. Come on, I saw you fooling in the garage this afternoon."

"I wasn't near the car."

"Yes, you were, buster. I heard the door slam all the way in the kitchen."

The boy caught the red edge of the sun along the knife. "Maybe it was Amy," he said languidly.

"It was you." Billy squatted down and opened the lid of the cigar box.

"Leave that alone!"

147

He dumped the contents in the dirt. A pack of cigarettes, matches. "Where'd you get the smokes?" he asked. "That why you sneak out here? So you can grab a puff without the old man knowing?"

The boy returned the objects to the box. "Go away," he said. "Go cook dinner."

Billy moved closer to him. "Where's the whisky? You got a bottle stashed away out here, too?"

"I don't like whisky."

"You sure as hell liked it last night."

Tod turned his head to look at him without moving his body, and Billy was reminded again of a ventriloquist dummy. "I don't like whisky."

Billy jabbed him on the chest. "Then what were you doin' at the bar last night? Looking at all the pretty bottles, reading the labels?" He laughed. "You might have a big blindfold tied over McGregor's eyes, but you ain't sneaking anything past Billy Easter. You have to get up awful early in the morning to do that."

"Go away," the boy said.

"Go where? You ordering me off my own place? I run this here hotel, buster. If you don't believe me just you go ask McGregor. Him and me got an agreement. So cough up those keys and stick to playing your games with the old man. They don't work with the big boys."

"I don't have any keys."

Billy took him by the shoulders, and the boy stiffened. "You don't, huh? Now, if I was to start shakin' you, you might change your tune. And if you don't like it, you can always go out that tunnel and down the road."

The boy's mouth dropped open, and his eyes widened.

"That got to you, didn't it?" Billy laughed, hoisting him up in the air. "I could see your eyes pop on that one. You better learn Billy Easter gets around. There ain't too much he misses."

148

He felt in the boy's shirt pocket. "What's in there? Feels like something metal." He reached in and removed the set of car keys. "Well how do you like that?" he said. "There they are, nice as you please."

He lowered Tod to the ground, and the boy balled his fists, his face cloudy with anger.

Far off near the house a voice cried, "Billy! It's time to start dinner." The smoke from the burning leaves had entered the little glen, mixing with the last light of the sun.

"Be right there," Billy called. For a second he turned away from the boy. When he looked back Tod had jumped over the ring of boxes and was running.

Billy's first instinct was to chase him. But it didn't matter now, he had the keys back. He could hear the boy's broken flight through the underbrush, the surprised chirp of birds. Let him run off and cry, he thought. What that kid needs is a good whipping, once a day, till he wises up. Now he knows who's boss around here.

Flames devoured the headless horse. The paint curled up, sizzling, like burning fat. Mr. McGregor moved away from the incinerator on the drive, the black smoke pouring past his head. He broke some of the toy train tracks and chucked them on the blaze.

It was a dull, overcast morning, rare for October, with clouds scudding in from the ocean. The children were upstairs in their bedroom playing with the newts.

A doll stared up at him from behind the wire mesh of the incinerator, then its head blew apart like a bubble, its glass eyes tinkling. Another doll was burning, and its plastic head crawled with fire.

"You wanted to see me?" Billy Easter said. He had come

out from the kitchen, a dish towel draped neatly over one broad shoulder.

The old man nodded, fascinated by the flames.

"I got work to do."

The last doll's head burst, a tiny pop like a light bulb. Then its fragments settled with the rest of the black dust to the bottom of the container. "Why did you go after Tod yesterday?" Mr. McGregor asked.

"Why did I do *what*?"

"You know exactly what I mean. You went out to that new fort he's building and intimidated him. You even tore his shirt."

"He actually *tell* you that?"

"I saw the shirt, Billy." Mr. McGregor tried to keep himself calm.

"Now wait just one sweet minute," the chauffeur said. "I didn't rip no shirt. I picked him up once and set him down. And that's *all*."

The old man poked at the ashes with one of the tracks. "His ankle was cut."

"So?"

"Billy, his *ankle* was cut."

"Maybe he fell down."

The old man felt his anger welling up. He brandished the section of track. "Don't lie to me! You put your hands on him."

"Get away with that thing," Billy said, bringing up his arm defensively. "You wanna poke my eye out or something?"

Mr. McGregor looked at the sharp prongs on the end of the track. He struggled for a moment to get his temper under control. When he spoke again his voice was level. "I'll ask you once more. Why did you go out there? What did you do to him?"

Billy jittered with frustration, glancing at the gray sky.

"Oh, man," he said. "Look—yesterday afternoon I checked the car. Okay? And the keys were missing. The kid had been playing in the garage, so I figured he took them."

Mr. McGregor regarded him with dismay. How could he lie so blatantly? "Now Billy, why would a boy of ten steal the car keys?"

"Why do kids do anything?"

"Are you suggesting that he wanted to drive the car?"

"Maybe he did it for spite. How should I know?"

The old man considered this. Perhaps Tod was angry with him because he was denied the birthday party. But that was patently ridiculous. The fury of children spent itself quickly—one moment they'd be screaming, hating you, but they could never sustain it. A moment later they'd be laughing, all anger forgotten. It was the nature of things. "Billy, can you *prove* he had the keys?"

"I can't prove nothing," the chauffeur said hotly. "There was nobody with us but the birds. They ain't learned to talk yet."

"Don't be sarcastic. Now I'll tell you what I think. I think the keys were in the car. They *remained* in the car. You had another reason for going after Tod."

"Get him down here," Billy demanded. "Ask him yourself while I'm lookin' at him."

"He's had a hard enough time as it is. For your information he was crying in his sleep last night. I heard him all the way in my bedroom."

"Crying!" Billy spat it out. "Man, that's just to suck you in." He suddenly pointed up at the house. "Look!"

Mr. McGregor followed the raised finger. Tod's face was in the bedroom window staring down at them.

"Spying on us," Billy said with triumph. "Next thing he'll say I ate their damn fish. And you'll believe it."

The face drew back, leaving a square of blank glass.

The old man shrugged. "He's interested. I told him I was

going to speak to you this morning."

Billy tossed him the dish towel. "Better tie that around your eyes. You're walking around half-blind anyway."

Mr. McGregor glared at him. "We'll talk about this later."

"Just one thing. What's *his* side? I mean, he's just sitting out there like Gentleman Jim, and I come up and knock him around. That it?"

"You were angry because he took those orange crates. You said he should have asked your permission."

Billy shook his head, then his face grew cold. "You better tell that boy to stay outta my sight."

"I'll do nothing of the kind." Mr. McGregor turned back to the dying fire. "Finish your work," he said. "And keep away from the children."

When he turned back he saw Billy stalking toward the kitchen, slapping his fists against his hips. He sighed to himself. Well, Loretta would know what to do with him. She would think of a solution.

Billy Easter listened at the playhouse door to the sound of ripping paper. The children were in the cabin exclaiming over some packages the old man had brought back from a shopping trip. "Mine's better than yours," the little girl said.

More sounds of crinkling paper. Billy looked back at the house. The heavy curtains were drawn against the old man's bedroom window; it was time for his afternoon nap.

"You look dumb," the boy said.

"So do you."

Billy stepped over to the porthole and peered inside. What he saw astounded him. The girl, amazingly, had transformed herself into a miniature nurse. She was wearing a cape, a stiff white apron, a blouse, and a tiny starched cap. The boy was getting into a policeman's uniform, buckling a pistol belt around his waist. At their feet were the empty cardboard boxes.

Billy's mind reeled, then he grinned. Halloween, he thought. Tonight was Halloween, he had seen it in the paper. Was that crazy old man going to let them roam the length of St. Cloud Road, ringing doorbells for trick or treat?

"That's not a real gun," the girl said, going to the mirror and admiring herself.

"Stay where you are. Don't move."

"It's a water pistol. Anybody can see that."

"Stand still," he threatened.

"Poo. I'll call Mr. McGregor."

"That won't do any good. He's dead. I shot him."

Billy Easter walked into the room. "Well, now," he said.

The boy showed a small flicker of annoyance. He deliberately turned his back and marched to the mirror to survey his new costume.

"Billy!" the girl cried. She ran swooping into his arms. "Take us for a ride, Billy."

"Can't," he said. "Got better things to do."

She stepped back so he could see the nurse's outfit. "Isn't it nice?"

"Beautiful. If I cut my finger will you fix it for me?"

"Of course." She showed him a little plastic first-aid kit that had come with the costume. Inside were packets of bandages, rolls of gauze, and a tiny bottle of candy shaped like aspirin.

Billy watched the boy in the mirror. He was spinning the gun around his finger, squinting at his policeman's profile under the pulled-down visor of the dark-blue cap. "Feeling pretty good, huh, Gentleman Jim?"

"You're not supposed to come near us," the boy said.

"You gonna run and tell the old man?"

"Maybe."

Billy patted the little girl on the head and went over to

the mirror. "Got it made, don't you?" he said, pushing the cap down over the boy's eyes.

Tod removed the cap. "Cut it out."

"No homework, lots of presents. I'd say you were doin' okay."

The boy made no comment. He pinned the gold badge on his tunic.

"Look at me," said Billy Easter.

The boy looked, impatiently. It was as if someone had pulled him away from the television set.

"Weren't you brought up right?" the chauffeur said, beginning to enjoy himself. "Didn't anybody teach you not to tell lies?"

"See?" said the little girl. She had placed at bandage across the forehead of her doll.

Billy didn't take his eyes from the boy's face. "Bet you don't like liars, do you?"

Tod shrugged.

Carefully, Billy brought his foot down on the boy's instep so that an increase of pressure would crack every bone. "I asked you a question, Gentleman Jim. I asked if you liked liars."

Tod's face had turned pale, but he didn't wince. "No," he said quietly.

"Good. That makes two of us."

Amy sat on a stool and watched them, chewing the cuticle on her thumb.

Billy kept up a constant pressure. "I'll tell you what you're gonna do. You're gonna go see McGregor. You're gonna tell him everything you said about me was a lie."

The boy tried to wriggle loose from the heavy foot. "No," he muttered.

"Yes," Billy said, pressing down. It was like stepping on a bird; it seemed so light, fragile. "You're gonna tell him you made the whole thing up."

"I can't! He's taking his nap."

"Boy, you really got excuses. Well then, you wait till after dinner when he's all filled with food. You wait till he lights up one of those big black cigars and starts soaking up the brandy."

"Are you mad, Billy?" the little girl asked.

"He'll never believe me," said Tod, biting his lip.

"Yes he will. You just tell him the plain simple truth."

"He'll punish me."

Billy smiled. "Maybe. That's the chance liars take, isn't it?"

"Let's go for a ride," Amy said.

"Well?" said Billy. "I'm waiting, Gentleman Jim. You gonna tell the old man or aren't you?"

"Suppose I don't?" The last words were barely audible. Tears had begun to form along the boy's clear, bright eyes.

"That's hard to say," Billy admitted. "I might lock you in that trunk over there for a couple days. Or, maybe I'll just press down with my foot. Like this." He exerted more pressure.

"All right!" Anger exploded in the boy's voice.

Billy removed his foot, grinning. "Figured you'd say that. Now I won't be around tonight. But I'm gonna check with the old man tomorrow morning. And if you haven't told him—"

The boy went down on one knee and massaged his foot. "I'll tell him," he said under his breath.

"You're still mad," said Amy. "I can tell."

"Me?" Billy laughed. "No *sir*. I'm the world's happiest guy."

"Take us for a ride."

Billy went to the door. "Can't. Gotta make dinner. Gotta put the caterpillar oil in the salad."

"Caterpillar oil!" the little girl marveled. She laughed and then began to sneeze.

Billy glanced at the boy. He was standing up, testing his weight experimentally on his foot. "Soak it in hot water," Billy advised. Then he squeezed through the door and flattened his hand like a starfish on the porthole glass. "Goodbye, little lady," he called. "You too, Gentleman Jim."

It was Friday morning. Mr. McGregor tumbled out of bed with an abundance of energy that surprised and delighted him. He felt like forty again, his appetite ravenous, his head as clear as spring water. Billy was already in the bedroom, using a brush on his gray Oxford with great crackling strokes.

When he went down to the kitchen the children were still eating breakfast, making loud slurping sounds with the milk in their cereal bowls. This morning the old man didn't mind; it seemed to complement his own bubbling vitality. "While I'm out," he instructed the children, "I want you to go over those school books I bought you."

Amy's blue eyes darkened. She shook her head.

"Darling," he said, "you and Tod must get back to your lessons. Do you want to grow up and be ignorant?"

"She's already ignorant," the boy commented.

"Shut up," snapped Amy. "Know what you are? You're a Mongolian idiot."

At a loss for something to do, for a way to occupy all of this new energy, Mr. McGregor busied himself by clearing up the breakfast dishes. Billy was off schedule this morning.

Tod came over to the sink. "How long will you be gone?"

"A few hours. And when I come back I'm going to have a nice surprise for you."

"An animal?" Amy asked.

"No," said the old man, beaming. "A person."

Tod frowned. "Who?"

156

"You'll see when I get back."

"Tell us now!" the little girl insisted.

"And spoil all the fun? No, you two get at your lessons, and before you know it, I'll be back with my surprise."

"You're mean," Amy cried.

Mr. McGregor finally escaped upstairs before they could pester him with more questions. The house today was like a badly run menagerie—cats underfoot in the kitchen, children gurgling symphonically with their milk—yet he found he enjoyed it. When he reached his bedroom Billy helped him on with his jacket. "Real sharp, Mr. McGregor," he said.

"Thank you, Billy. I take it that's a compliment."

"Sure is."

The old man observed himself in the mirror. Excellent. Loretta would be pleased by the sight of him. He sprinkled some extra shaving lotion on his face as Billy fashioned a handkerchief into a neat crown of points and tucked it into his breast pocket.

"Where are you going?" the chauffeur asked.

"I'm bringing my daughter home."

Billy made no comment.

Perhaps he thinks it strange that I have a daughter, the old man thought. He'd better get used to the idea.

Downstairs, the children were running fresh water in a bowl for the newts. "This one's called Sparkle," Amy said. "And that one's Sam."

"How can you tell them apart?" he asked.

She grinned guiltily at him. "I can't."

He reminded them again of their homework, then went out to the garage. He saw the playhouse through Loretta's eyes; she would be dazzled. As he was opening the car door Billy came quickly from the house. "I won't be needing you," he said. "I'll drive it myself. You can dust the living room."

157

Billy hesitated, something on his mind. Then he said, "Tod talk to you last night?"

"Tod? About what?"

"The car keys."

"I thought we cleared that up. There was nothing to discuss."

Billy seemed disturbed. "He didn't talk to you at all?"

"No." Impatient, eager to get started, Mr. McGregor abruptly climbed behind the wheel. He backed the car onto the drive, leaving Billy standing by the entrance to the garage. A small finger of uncertainty began to prod him. Was he doing the right thing? The children would be alone in the house with Billy, and the man obviously harbored a grudge. Perhaps he should go back, take them with him.

The gates swung up and he braked. No—it would be awkward with the children at the sanitarium. Questions, stares; it was too risky. He could take Billy with him, of course, but who would watch over the children? They had never been alone for more than an hour or two. Better to leave them in Billy's charge. He climbed out of the car and opened the gates, telling himself there was nothing to worry about.

Something was going on. There was an unusual amount of congestion at the corner of Sunset Boulevard. An accident? Several police cars seemed to be cruising, one of them with its red light whirling. For a terrifying instant he thought they had come for him. They were going to storm the estate and rescue the children. But their movements were so aimless and erratic that he was able to relax. Whatever they were doing had no relation to him or his secret.

When he reached the ocean the sky was a brilliant, scalding blue—yet back toward the boulevard, in the general vicinity of Bel-Air, there seemed to be a gradual darkening of the atmosphere. Perhaps a storm was building up, one of those tropical things that came lashing out of nowhere, choking the canyons with torrents of muddy water, tearing the leaves from great royal palms like petals from a dandelion. The last one he could recall was years ago. He remembered huddling in the house with Loretta and the children on a noon black as night, the phone wires down, the electricity disrupted. They had lit candles and sang Easter hymns (it was Palm Sunday), and Ruthie's frightened crying had been drowned out by the continuous crash of waterfalls on the roof. He also remembered, guiltily, that he had rather liked the storm. It reminded him of home, his real home, where rainstorms weren't freak accidents, but were sometimes even welcomed. His father always said they were good for the soil and good for the soul.

Well, let it come, he thought philosophically. Lord knows they needed rain; months had passed without a drop. He snapped on the radio and found a station that was playing a string quartet. The measured music calmed him, it made him think, for no real reason, of a towering medieval church on a great sunlit square, orderly files of monks in black.

As he drove farther north, the day grew brighter, the ocean unmarked by sails or foam. He realized he should have brought his sunglasses along. There wasn't a cloud in the sky. He headed up into the hills toward the little park and its sanitarium, and as he came closer he felt his palms begin to sweat. Steady, he told himself. You simply want to take your daughter for a ride. They can't deny you that.

He drove into the lot, parked, and walked slowly toward the main building. The Good Humor man was on the lawn again, and he had a sudden craving for some ice cream. He bought a pineapple Popsicle, tore away the frozen paper, and bit ferociously into the cold bar.

In the booming lobby he waited by the reception desk while the same cigarette-smoking nurse gave directions to an elderly couple weighted down with bouquets of wild, roadside flowers. The mathematics of the string quartet soared through his mind.

"Yes?" the nurse asked. She caught him at the very moment when he dropped a small shard of ice on her desk.

"Sorry." He quickly brushed it off. Another spot fell to his jacket.

"Can I help you?" the woman said, plainly annoyed by his clumsiness.

"Is Dr. Stauderman here? I'd like to talk with him."

"I'll see," she said, turning to her telephone.

Damn. He picked at the tiny yellow spot already melting into his lapel. He hadn't wanted to look seedy and unkempt today.

The nurse cradled the phone. "If you'll wait over there the doctor will be right out."

"Thank you. Thanks very much." He sat down with the other visitors and crossed his legs, trying to look like a respectable businessman taking a few precious hours off to see a relative. He dropped the half-eaten Popsicle into a waste receptacle near the wall.

Waiting. It was like his trips to Norman's office, meetings that neither of them wanted. Here at least he was anonymous, just another face in the lobby. What would Stauderman say? I'm afraid it's impossible, Mr. McGregor. Your daughter hasn't been feeling well; she didn't even touch her creamed corn. Why don't you come back next month? A drive, Mr. McGregor? Why do you want to take her for a drive? May I see your hands? Why are you sweating so much?

He rubbed his palms against his trousers. The music had left him. He was very aware now of sounds; the endless shuffle of feet in the lobby, the talk that floated down like

160

feathers from the upstairs rooms. It was as if he was waiting in a vast railroad terminal in a city where he was a stranger. If only he had a timetable to study, gray rows of arrivals and departures to soothe his eyes.

Stauderman came from a side door carrying a clipboard. Today he didn't look like a doctor; he was wearing a turtleneck sweater with patches at the elbows and jeans. Where does he think he is? the old man reflected angrily. Getting ready for a card game with some friends?

"Mr. McGregor. How are you?" the young man said, shifting the clipboard so they could shake hands.

"Just fine." He hid the spot on his lapel with his finger. "I didn't recognize you in that outfit." Good, he thought, put him on the defensive.

Stauderman smiled. "Had an emergency this morning. Haven't had time to change." He tapped the clipboard against his thigh. "Shall we go and see your daughter?"

"No, not quite yet," Mr. McGregor said, steeling himself. The man's cool gaze lingered questioningly on his face, and he forced himself to continue. "Do you remember the last time I was here? I asked you if I could take her out for a ride?"

The doctor nodded, noncommittal.

"I was thinking," he went on, stumbling, "I was thinking that today would be perfect. I don't know if you've been out, but the weather's beautiful."

"Certainly is," said Stauderman, looking slightly amused.

"It would only be for a few hours. A nice long drive in the sun and then lunch at one of those seafood restaurants on the highway. Loretta always liked crab salad." He felt compelled to keep talking, saturate the empty seconds with sound, anything to push away Stauderman's silence. "There's a gift shop not far from here—they sell a lot of junk, actually—but they have a wonderful collection of seashells and things like that and I thought...."

Stauderman nodded gravely. "And you thought...?"

"Well, I thought it might interest her, if you know what I mean. All she sees is that room and that television set." He paused and shot a guarded look at the young man. He was still in a listening attitude, his head cocked to one side as if he were thoroughly engrossed and quite prepared to go on listening all morning. What are you up to? the old man thought, rubbing his hands against his trousers. Did he catch that movement? Let me see your palms, Mr. McGregor. Smiling while he looked at the telltale sweat.

"What do you think?" the old man asked.

Stauderman was still nodding in a preoccupied way, as if something else had occurred to him, something that had nothing to do with Loretta. "Uh-huh," he said, "yeah. Could you come back to my office a minute."

"Well—yes. But I wanted to know—"

"Won't take long."

The old man followed him, his eyes on the swinging clipboard. What was going on? Who did he have back there in those hidden offices? A battery of other young doctors? He could picture a group of them sitting around with coffee, nodding at him and asking questions, saying "yeah" and "uh-huh," all of them dressed in turtleneck sweaters and jeans.

Stauderman's office was a cubbyhole with a metal desk and two chairs. A clerk's office, really, the old man thought with disappointment. Where were his framed diplomas, degrees? But no one else was there. Good.

The young man switched on the overhead light and dropped down behind the desk. "Cigarette?" he asked, extending a crumpled pack.

"No, no thanks. I'm a cigar man." He tried to smile.

"Smart," Stauderman said. "My wife told me to give them up, or she'd divorce me." He looked at the pack ruefully and then removed a cigarette, sticking it in the

162

corner of his mouth. "Please, sit down. Sorry I don't have a cigar for you, but nobody smokes them around here."

The old man took a seat, relieved that the chair faced the window instead of the doctor.

"Relax. I'm not going to take your blood pressure."

Mr. McGregor laughed. It sounded terrible to him, more like a moan. "Always disliked doctor's offices," he said. "They make me nervous."

Stauderman leaned back in his chair and linked his sweatered arms behind his neck. "Mr. McGregor," he said, "you seem rather keyed-up about this—if you don't mind my saying so."

The old man sank deeper in his chair, feeling a vein in his temple begin to tremble. Here it comes, he thought, wanting to shut his eyes. "I do?" he choked out.

"It's almost as if—how shall I put it?—the idea of coming here and taking your daughter away is compulsive. And I think I know why."

The old man squirmed. "Oh?"

"You probably believe that a new atmosphere—gift shops, restaurants—might produce a sudden change, something concrete that you'll be able to put your finger on. And that's not a realistic attitude, I'm afraid. It's important that you don't expect too much."

"No, really, I'm not expecting much at all. I only felt that she needed a change of scene."

"I hope you're being honest with me. Loretta has shown some improvement but it's gradual, we measure it in degrees. An afternoon's outing would be pleasant for her, but there won't be any miracles. She needs extended professional care."

"Of course, of course, I understand perfectly."

"Good. I just don't want you to be disappointed."

The old man held his hands steady in his lap. "And—it's all right if I take her out for a few hours?"

"I don't see why not." Stauderman took a pencil from his desk and pulled over a pad. "What's your son-in-law's telephone number?"

"My son-in-law?" The little pulse in his temple jumped again.

"I'll have to ask his permission. He's responsible, you know. We don't like to do anything without approval."

Norman. Norman would throw cold water on everything. Was this to be the barrier, the one unforeseeable element he hadn't planned on? "I—spoke to him myself," he stammered. "He said it's fine with him."

"Better call him anyway," the doctor said smoothly. "What's the number?"

"But he already gave me—"

"I know, but I'm the attending physician. One of our rules."

Mr. McGregor stood up. "I don't remember it offhand."

The young man reached out for the phone and dialed. "Jenny," he said, "get me a listing for a Mr. Norman Abbott—no, wait—" he glanced at the old man. "What's the name of your company?"

Mr. McGregor stood by the window. A few feet below was a bed of azaleas, rippled and pleated by the wind into yellow silk. His wife had loved azaleas, or had it been Loretta?

"Mr. McGregor? The name of your company?"

If he opened the window it might be possible to grab a handful.

Stauderman scraped back his chair. "Is something wrong?"

"No. Just a touch of dizziness." He brought his burning hands to his face. "McGregor Bathing Suits. In Santa Monica."

"Jenny," the doctor said to the phone, "McGregor Bathing Suits. Santa Monica."

The old man groped back to the chair and sat down again.

164

"Would you like a glass of water?"

"It was just a passing spell. I'm fine."

Stauderman brought the phone to his ear and poised his pencil. "Thank you, Jenny. No. I'll ring it myself."

Where were they?

Billy Easter was systematically searching the house. When he had come in after talking to the old man he discovered they were gone and assumed that they had fled to some nook or cranny and were hiding from him.

First he ransacked the basement, pushing away towers of dusty bric-a-brac, brushing his face against the cool curtains of spiderwebs that hung from the rusted waterpipes. How had the old man ever accumulated so much junk: straw sewing baskets like overgrown bird nests, broken clocks, barrels bursting with books, and ironing boards. He had heard nothing while he hunted, not a creak or suspicious shuffle.

Now he searched the living room, checking behind the chairs and sofa. At the bar he paused for a few swallows of rum. It spread fire in his stomach, reminding him that in his hurry to find the children he had neglected breakfast. He looked behind the curtains; nothing but some anthills of dust and a mouse that blinked red eyes at him.

He went into the closed-off dining room and snapped the switch for the two crystal lamps over the sideboard. They didn't light, and he could only blame himself for not replacing the bulbs. But it was really the old man's fault, he decided—he had moved his life into a few rooms and forgotten about the others.

Grumbling, Billy crouched down, swept away the stiff lace dinner cloth, and peered under the long table. Then it occurred to him that they might have locked themselves in the playhouse. No, they didn't have a key, and the house offered more room for concealment. He moved down the back hallway. Its bulb was also burned out, but he could see a long dark tongue of stain on the ceiling. Several months ago the old man had fallen asleep in his bathtub and a portion of the upstairs hallway had been flooded. Lucky we both weren't drowned, he thought.

No one had entered the library in almost a year. Dust stung his nostrils, and he stumbled about in the dark, catching his ankle on a heavy piece of furniture. He went to the windows and ripped away the thick, brocaded curtains. The rod snapped and the curtains dropped down on him like a sail, sending up a smoke screen of dust. Sneezing, he worked himself free. There were little diamond panes in the windows, ruby-colored and aquamarine, and the filtered sun pushed a prism of light against the wall of old books and the threadbare Persian rug. The only place to hide was a closet near the door. He opened it and laughed when he found another ironing board.

This is stupid, he thought, feeling his way down the hall again. He could make himself a sandwich, load it on a paper plate with some pickles and olives, and enjoy lunch while he searched. It wasn't a bad idea, but it was too much trouble.

He mounted the steps and went into the first bedroom at the foot of the upper hall. Now what's this? he wondered, as the door swung silently back and tapped the wall. The room was spic and span, smelling of furniture polish. It looked like a woman's place, with a fancy dressing table and a deep four-poster bed with a big canopy decorated with a shower of lavender tassels. Ain't this something, he whistled. He sat down on the mattress, bouncing his hips. No dirt anywhere. McGregor must have been at work, cleaning up and using the vacuum. Why would he go to so much trouble with just one room and leave all the others alone?

He checked under the bed and opened two large closets which were stuffed with women's coats and dresses, dozens of shoes pocketed in a mat on the wall. Then he went back into the hall again, heading for the old man's bedroom. Maybe they're not here, he thought. Maybe they took off for the boy's fort in the woods. He'd get to that later.

The bedroom was just as he had left it, pajamas and dressing gown on the floor, the air full of the bay rum scent the old man rubbed on his cheeks. He went into the bathroom and inspected the old-fashioned tub. Dry as an empty well. Ever since it had spilled over McGregor never used it, preferring a sponge bath at the sink.

Damn those kids! he thought, wishing he had brought the bottle upstairs with him. Where were they? And then he heard a sound—a whisper, low and guarded. He crept back into the sunny bedroom and moved to the doors of the wall-length, built-in closet. Had the whisper come from there?

He slid open one of the doors, its coaster squeaking along the metal track. Tod and Amy stood inside against the dark rows of coats and jackets, looking up at him with innocent eyes. The boy wore his policeman's costume and the girl her nurse's outfit. They didn't say a word.

Billy backed up a step, confused. Other kids would have tried to dodge around him and run away, but they just stood there in those crazy costumes as if they expected him to make their lunch. "What are you doin' in there all dressed up?" he said, his voice loud in the hushed room. "Halloween's over."

They remained in the closet. He had the strange feeling that if he closed the sliding door they wouldn't much care. A shirt had fallen loose from the shelf and its arm dangled on the little girl's cap.

"Out," he said. "Come on, move!"

They walked into the bedroom. Billy closed the door and

turned to the boy. "You and me got something to settle, Gentleman Jim."

Tod nodded. Amy wandered to the aquarium where the old man's fish hung in the water.

"That all you can do, shake your head? You said you'd talk to McGregor last night. Isn't that what you told me?"

The boy nodded again.

"He says you didn't do it. How come?"

Tod put his hand in his pocket and brought it out again. The fingers were curled in a loose fist.

"What are you doin'?"

The fingers snapped open. A small green wad, not much larger than a postage stamp, sat on the boy's palm. Billy picked it off and opened it up. His breath suddenly caught in his throat as he smoothed out the folds. It was a much-wrinkled hundred dollar bill. "Where'd you get this?" he asked.

The boy lifted a shoulder. His hand disappeared in his pocket again. When it came out the fingers were lightly cupped.

Another one?

The fingers opened slowly, as if Tod were performing a magic trick, and Billy could see a tiny green ball. The boy juggled it for a moment, then let it roll off his palm to the floor. Billy squatted down and scrambled for the bill. As he twisted it open, he noticed that the children were still wearing their bedroom slippers.

"Gitty-up," the little girl said. She had climbed up on his back as he crouched over the tile floor on all fours.

"Not now, honey," he said.

"Gitty-up, horsie," she commanded, rapping his neck.

This one was a fifty. It gave off an odd aroma, and he pressed it to his nose. Camphor! Where had he smelled camphor-scented money before? Sure—the night McGregor had locked him in the kitchen and gone to the place where he hid his money.

He arched his back slightly, and Amy slid, protesting, to the floor. Tod was looking down at him, his face eager. "Give us both a ride," he said.

"Where'd you get this stuff?"

"Give us both a ride."

Billy started to rise, but the girl had taken hold of his shirt and was mounting his back again. "Around the room, Billy," she giggled imperiously.

"All right, just once," he said, gathering up the bills and firmly planting his hands and knees on the floor. The boy hopped on, straddling his back behind the girl.

"Gitty-up," Amy cried, smacking him on the hip.

Billy twisted his neck to look at Tod. "You're gonna show me where that money is," he said.

"After you give us a ride."

"How much is there?"

"Gitty-up," Tod cried. Amy pounded his side.

Billy started to move. Goddamn they were heavy! The girl wasn't bad, but the boy sat on him with all his weight, pressing him down. He crawled around the side of the bed, dragging in air through his open mouth.

"Faster," Amy ordered. Her hand struck him sharply under his heart.

Sweet Jesus, he thought. I should've poked that boy and made him show me where the money is. He went across the room to the door, then back to the bed, and finally he rolled over, tossing them to the floor.

"That wasn't enough," said Amy.

"End of the line," he breathed. "Next time get a real horse." The boy was starting to move away, and he took hold of his ankle. "Where is it?"

"I have to go to the bathroom."

"It'll hold. You got your ride, and now I get my money."

"Don't show him," the little girl said. She tried to mount his back again but he pushed her away.

The boy removed another green ball from his pocket. In the warm light of the bedroom it looked like a gumdrop. "Go get it, horsie," he said, flipping it through the door.

Billy moved like lightning. The ball lay on the carpet in the hallway, and he scooped it up. Tod ran out, brushing past him; he held another ball high over his head like a prize. He tossed it toward the stairway.

"Hey! Stop playin' games," Billy shouted, diving after it. It rolled down the steps, and he almost tripped, grabbing at the newel post at the bottom of the landing. The hallway was dark, shot through with streaks of light, but the little ball had vanished. He felt along the carpet as the boy came slowly down the stairs, holding his sister by the hand.

Billy finally found the money and stuffed it in his pocket. "You through having your fun?" he asked. He wanted to twist the boy's arm behind his back, but that wouldn't be smart under the circumstances.

Tod walked into the living room and went to the bar.

"Hold on," Billy said, following him. "No drinking, understand? You wanna drink, do it at night."

The boy was carefully removing bottles from the shelf and setting them on the floor. What's this? the chauffeur puzzled. Why's he clearing all those bottles away?

"I'm hungry, Billy," the little girl said.

"Later."

He watched as Tod opened a hinged metal panel built into the lower part of the shelving. It swung back to reveal a small safe. "Well now," he said, brushing the boy away and spinning the combination wheels. "How'd you find this?"

"I looked."

"That what you were doing here a couple nights ago? Trying to get in this thing?"

The child's expression was proud. "I told you I didn't drink."

"And I believe you," Billy grinned. "I had you figured all wrong. You're about half smart, Gentleman Jim."

Tod took a scrap of paper from his pocket, glanced at it, and then began spinning the wheels. His fingers moved rapidly, as if guided by long habit.

Billy was fascinated. "Where'd you get that paper?" he asked.

"He keeps it hidden. I found it."

Billy laughed aloud and punched him playfully on the arm. "How do you like that? Here I been looking for this thing for almost a year, and it takes a little squirrel like you to show me where it is."

The boy clicked the door open, and Billy made a small noise in his throat, clearing it. He nibbled at his dry lower lip as he looked at the stacks of currency and securities. It was like peering into a cave; it made something flutter in the bottom of his stomach. "How much would you say there is?" he asked in a subdued voice.

"Don't know."

He dug out one of the stacks of bills. It felt like a bar of gold, as heavy as a phone directory. He riffled the corners, the denominations blurring. Hundreds of dollars. And there were three more packets in the drawer.

"Keep it," the boy said.

Billy gaped at him. The money meant no more to Tod than a stack of old newspapers. "You take any of this?" he asked.

"Just the ones I rolled up."

Billy uncapped a bottle of rum on the floor and took a quick swallow. He still felt light-headed so he took another.

He put the bundle back in the safe.

Tod was surprised. "Don't you want it?" he asked.

"I didn't say that. How come you're showing me all this? How come you haven't salted it away in a hollow tree or something?"

The boy shrugged. "You wanted to see it."

"Make us tuna fish sandwiches," the girl said. She tugged at his arm.

Billy turned away from the safe, thinking. He didn't have to take the whole amount—just some of it. No reason to clean McGregor out. When you came right down to it, the old man had been pretty generous with him. Just some of it.

"Well?" the boy said. He stood straight as a sentry at the open safe.

Billy's mind was swimming. He saw his hut, made of solid brick instead of straw. Ladies handbags, alligator-skin shoes and Gucci wallets. A beach full of rum bottles, gleaming under the moon like loaves of bread. No more crawling down a tunnel every night; no more cooking meals for other people. He could buy a one-way plane ticket that afternoon and be touching down over the Caribbean the next night. And nobody would care. The old man sure as hell didn't want him here.

"Nothing grows on you, Gentleman Jim," he said, licking his thumb and peeling off bills. He counted the small packet he had taken. Almost four thousand dollars. That would do the trick with plenty to spare. He'd have to buy some new clothes—couldn't board that plane in his used rags. He put the money in his pocket and started for the archway.

"Where are you going?" the little girl asked.

"Home."

Tod closed the safe and spun the wheels. "Where's that?"

"Long away from here, that's for sure."

"But what about our tuna fish sandwiches?" said Amy.

"Mr. McGregor'll fix you lunch. He'll be back soon." Should he pack his things, take his suitcase? No. He'd go just the way he came, with nothing.

The children followed him to the front door. He tried to tousle Tod's hair, but the boy pulled away. "You kids listen to that old man," he said. "Do what he tells you."

"Will you bring us a present when you come back?" asked Amy.

He grinned. "When I come back I'll bring your great grandchildren presents. How's that?" He stepped through the door, hesitated, then waved to them. The little girl waved back, jumping up and down. Tod had gone into the house.

Billy thrust his face to the warm sky. It was a beautiful day but there was a funny smell in the air. Smog? He loped down the path to the tunnel, tucking the money in tighter next to his bone. You been good to me, bone, he thought. Now just get me safe and sound on that plane tonight.

Whistling, excited, Billy Easter ran down St. Cloud Road. He never looked back.

"He wants to talk to you," Dr. Stauderman said, extending the receiver.

Mr. McGregor reluctantly took it. Why hadn't he kept that luncheon appointment with his son-in-law? Why had he lied to the doctor about getting his permission? "Hello, Norman," he croaked into the phone. Stauderman was leaning back in his chair, the pencil tapping against his knee.

"Dad," Norman said, "how are you? Listen, I think it's a good idea, taking Loretta out for a ride."

"You do?" The old man was rattled by the unexpected approval.

"The last time I was up there she was so pale I wanted to get her a sunlamp."

"Yes—I thought the same thing."

"But I wouldn't take her far. A few miles, like the doctor said. Tell Billy to drive slowly. Let her enjoy the scenery."

"Of course." He glanced at Stauderman. The doctor was doodling on his pad, looking bored.

"By the way, I called you last week. Around ten at night. Nobody answered."

"I suppose I was out."

"You mean you're taking my advice? I don't believe it."

"There—was an interesting film in the Village."

"Good for you. You ought to do it more often. Next we're going to get you on a cruise. I know a travel agent. . . ."

The younger man chattered on, and Mr. McGregor found himself stifling a yawn. Amazing. A moment ago he had been afraid, dreading Norman's anger; now he just wanted to get him off the phone. "Yes, perhaps I'll call him."

His son-in-law caught the impatience in his voice. "Well, I guess you want to see Loretta. I won't keep you."

"Thank you, Norman."

"Thanks for what? Tell her I'll be up there one of these weekends. And let's definitely get together for lunch one of these days. You keep putting it off."

"We will. That's a promise."

The old man cradled the phone. It had been so simple. Why had he even bothered to worry?

"Shall we see her?" Stauderman said, rising.

The porch overlooked the ocean, a warm windy strip protected by lowered awnings and a high guard rail. A few patients strolled its length, light coats thrown over their bathrobes. Gulls dropped down into the sea like falling snowflakes.

"Should she be out here alone?" Mr. McGregor asked as

they entered from the second floor ward.

"She's not alone."

Loretta was at the far end of the porch sitting in a flimsy-looking aluminum chair. She was wearing sunglasses and a tan raincoat over a red wool dress, her hair drawn back under a scarf. A nurse stood behind her.

"Hello," the old man said. He touched her shoulder.

"Hello." She didn't bother to look at him. Her face in the bright light was bony, hollows under both cheeks. She wore no makeup.

"Enjoying the view?"

"The sea gulls have yellow beaks. I never noticed that before." She glanced at Stauderman. "Do you have a cigarette?"

"Now, Loretta, you know there's no smoking out here," he said. "Fire rule."

Mr. McGregor pulled over another aluminum chair and sat down. Why didn't the others go away? Why did they always hover close by with their listening faces? "It's certainly a lovely day," he said. "Be a shame wasting it indoors, wouldn't it?"

She pointed to a diving gull. "What do they look for down there?"

"Loretta, how would you like to go for a drive?"

"I don't think so," she said, sliding her hands into the pockets of the raincoat.

"But why not?" Baffled, he looked at Stauderman.

She didn't seem to hear. With the glare of light on her sunglasses, her lips tightly compressed, she seemed inaccessible.

Stauderman moved to the railing. "Any special reason, Loretta?"

"No."

Mr. McGregor felt cheated. It was the one thing he hadn't expected: his daughter's flat refusal.

"You just want to sit here all day?" Stauderman asked. "Watching the gulls?"

"What do they look for in the waves?" she said.

"Loretta," the old man said, "suppose we go for a walk around the garden?" If he could only get her alone, he could tell her about the children.

"I don't like to walk," she said. "It makes me tired." She pressed a hand to her eyes under the sunglasses.

"Do you want to go in now, Mrs. Abbott?" the nurse asked. Her voice was solicitous.

The old man turned frantically to the doctor. Once in the room, her gaze on the television set, she would be lost to him.

"I think Mrs. Abbott wants to enjoy the view a bit longer," Stauderman said, signalling the nurse. "Don't you, Loretta?"

"Yes."

Mr. McGregor's mind spun. How could he tempt her? What could he dredge up from their shared past to wheedle her acceptance? He suddenly remembered an art exhibit in Laguna, years ago, where they had wandered past rows of paintings in the open streets. She had bought something, and Norman criticized her selection. What was it? Yes—a collage, a peacock composed of scraps of glass. "We once went to an art exhibit," he said aloud. "Do you remember?"

She was silent, but he noticed that her hands emerged from her pockets. "Paintings?" she asked.

"Yes, paintings." Stauderman was motioning to him to go ahead, to keep trying. Funny, he thought, he really wants to help me. "We drove down to Laguna Beach. Norman was with us. Remember?"

She looked at him blankly.

"Of course you do. You bought a picture—it was made of glass. Pieces from old vases and perfume bottles."

She moved slightly in the chair, her hands fluttering.

"The peacock," she whispered. "The peacock with the tail of colored glass."

"Right!" He was overjoyed. "Well—the artist who painted it, he has a new exhibit only a few miles from here."

"I liked his work," she said, twisting a button on her coat. "Everything made of glass."

Stauderman leaned close to her. "Wouldn't you like to see more of his pictures?"

Say yes, the old man thought. Please say yes.

She seemed indecisive. The button came loose in her fingers.

"Here, let me have it," said the nurse. "We'll sew it back on."

Mr. McGregor wanted to order her off the porch so she wouldn't distract his daughter.

Loretta looked at the button, a small, discolored coin in her beautifully manicured hand. "I don't know," she said.

"We'll have a good time," said the old man. "Really we will."

"All right. It doesn't matter."

Mr. McGregor half-turned away; he didn't want Stauderman to see his relief. He cast his eyes to the ocean and saw the sun dance over the water.

"...then we'd better get you ready," the doctor was saying. "Do you want to go to your room and comb your hair?"

Miles of mellow sky. The seascape streamed by outside, broken by patches of rock and riotous redwood bungalows. Loretta sat close to the door, one leg tucked under her skirt, hands laced on her lap. She stared down at the dashboard as if the sky were an enemy. "Where are the paintings?" she asked.

"I have to stop at the house first." He knew that once she saw what he had waiting for her, she'd forgive him the necessary lie about the art exhibit.

He increased their speed to sixty, racing past stretches of beach and clapboard seafood restaurants thrusting out signs like arms. He wondered what the children were doing. It was early afternoon, and they were probably in the play-house. Billy would be standing over the kitchen sink, wash-ing and drying the dishes.

"The house?" Loretta said suddenly. *"Your* house?"

"Our house. Don't you remember it?" He paused, then added, "Where you brought Mark and Ruthie up."

He watched her lips move as she tasted the names. "Is Mark doing any better in school?"

"Yes. Much better. He brought home an excellent report card."

She smiled and it startled him—the gentle curve of her mouth, the white of her teeth. It was so lovely he turned away. "I'm glad he's doing better," she said.

He drummed his fingers on the wheel. Should he tell her about the children, prepare her? No, it should be a surprise to the very end. And she'd be delighted, he was sure of it. In the coming weeks, he'd gradually increase the number of "drives." She'd grow used to the children and the house, she'd even begin to take charge as her habit patterns re-turned. If things worked out, he'd obtain her permanent release from the institution. There would be a problem with Norman, of course, getting his permission, but there was plenty of time to think of a way to arrange it.

"Why do the birds hunt in the water?" she said.

He smiled. "Perhaps they're hungry."

She rested against the seat, and he put his arm around her. He felt like the White Rabbit, guiding Alice safely home.

THE PLAYHOUSE

* * *

They drove up the hill to the house. Don't you recognize these old trees? he thought. You played among them as a child; I made you a swing in that elm over there. Don't you remember your lawn party when you were sixteen? Young boys in stiff suits, dainty little girls in skirts like bells. I'll wager if you search through the bushes you'll find some of your old toys: skates and dolls buried under bushels of grass. Perhaps we'll go looking for them some afternoon.

"This is really your house?" she asked as he led her from the car.

"Yours, too." He wished that she would recognize something, a stone on the drive, the carved fleur-de-lis on the door. But her eyes remained blank.

When they entered, he called for Billy, but no one answered him. What had happened here? The living room was disheveled, chairs out of place, and the sofa moved away from the wall. Why was the library door open? He checked and found dusty diamonds of light from the bare panes shining on the folds of curtains which were lying on the floor. The house was topsy-turvy.

Loretta waited in the living room, her head lifted to the beamed ceiling, her body revolving in a circle. He stood in the library doorway and watched her, the disorder forgotten. Her sunglasses had fallen down to the bridge of her nose, and her cloudy eyes were examining the objects around her. Good, he thought, holding himself perfectly still. The house was working on her—slowly, slowly—draping her with its familiar sights and smells. Give it time, he thought. Let it seep over you.

Skipper ran in from the kitchen. He blundered around Loretta's legs, sniffing, almost as baffled as she was. Who was this strange young woman in the living room?

Have you forgotten her? the old man thought with dismay. Doesn't the perfume give you a hint? Perhaps the dog's nose, like its eyes, was failing.

Loretta bent down and stroked him. "Good dog," she said, petting his ears. Skipper growled and backed away from her.

"Skipper!" he rebuked the animal. "Let her pet you. What's wrong with you?"

"Skipper..." she whispered, echoing him. The dog nuzzled the old man, still growling low in its throat. "Skipper..." she repeated, revolving slowly under the rafters. The name gnawed at her, but the house had caught her again with its frail memories.

"He's our dog," Mr. McGregor said with urgency. "Mark picked him out in that pet store. Don't you remember?"

"Yes. I think so." She was distracted by a side table, a huge, solid piece of furniture with ornately carved legs. "This..." she said, feeling the top like a blind person fingering braille.

"Your mother bought it in Mexico City. You were eighteen. It was your graduation present—the trip."

"I don't remember."

"What about this?" he said, thrusting a heavy metal table lighter at her. She had given it to him for his birthday.

The eyes peered down over the sunglasses. "No."

Mr. McGregor almost felt like giving up. Seeing the old familiar room as his daughter probably saw it depressed him; it changed into something alien and uncharted as he watched. Even Skipper was a stranger. Who was this animal wandering through the house? He almost questioned his own right to be there.

"Where are they?" she asked.

Surprised, he turned to her. She rarely asked positive questions. "Who?" he said.

180

"My children." She removed the sunglasses, and her eyes probed him. Norman's eyes.

"I don't know," he admitted.

"School?" She looked at her wrist, but she wore no watch.

"No," he said awkwardly. "They . . . haven't been going."

"They're sick? Both of them?"

"No. No, they're fine." He found himself wishing she'd put the sunglasses back on. "They're probably playing somewhere."

She took off her raincoat and dropped it on the sofa. Ruthie's doll lay on one of the cushions. "Didn't I tell her?" she said, picking it up. "She insists on leaving this all over the house."

"I've told her myself," said the old man.

"Mark!" she called. "Ruthie!"

"I'll get them," he said. "Stay here. I'll go and find them." Where was Billy? He was supposed to clean up the living room, and it was a shambles.

He went into the kitchen, and he could hear the quick hammer of her high heels behind him. The refrigerator door was open and crumbs and dirty dishes covered the table.

"Where are they?" she repeated from behind him. "Mark knows he's to put his dishes on the drain board."

Mr. McGregor was furious at Billy. Couldn't the man be responsible for anything?

"Maybe they're in their room," Loretta said.

The old man suddenly realized where they were. The playhouse. That's where they spent their early afternoons. "Stay here," he said. "I'l get them."

Loretta nodded and began carrying the dirty dishes to the sink.

He hurried across the yard to the playhouse, scooping up one of Amy's toys on the way. There was a peculiar smell in the air, something acrid that irritated the little hairs inside his nostrils. Perhaps someone in the neighborhood was burning leaves again. He climbed the steps to the bridge and knocked sharply on the closed cabin door. "Tod?"

When no one answered, he pulled it open and peered into the half-lit room. Amy was sitting on one of the stools, still dressed in her nurse's uniform, her arms and legs bound with a heavy coil of sailor's rope. Her teeth nibbled at a handkerchief tied around her mouth, and the blue eyes stared at him with alarm.

"Amy!" he cried, stumbling toward her. "Who did this to you?" He unknotted the handkerchief with shaky fingers and worked on the ropes. "Are you all right?"

She turned her face to him, and he could see that she was smiling, a wide, ecstatic grin that revealed a missing tooth. A laugh bubbled up in her throat.

"What's wrong with you?" he said. "Why are you all tied up like this?"

Something rustled on the other side of the room. Tod was creeping toward him with his gun raised. He was wearing the policeman's uniform, a dark-blue little figure that moved in broken, surreptitious steps.

Amy laughed in his ear.

"Put that down," he said to the boy. "Why are you still wearing that costume?"

Tod stopped in front of him, sighting along the pistol with great concentration.

"What did you do to your sister?" the old man said crossly.

"She's my prisoner," said Tod.

Mr. McGregor loosened the rest of the knots. "No more games with rope. I want that clearly understood. You'll hurt each other."

Amy rubbed her wrists. "We were only playing," she said.

"You've been very naughty, both of you. You left all your lunch dishes on the table, and the refrigerator door was wide open." He paused. "Where's Billy?"

Tod lowered the gun. "We haven't seen him."

"What do you mean, you haven't seen him? Is he in the house?"

The boy was about to answer, but he suddenly looked past the old man and drew in his breath. Amy followed his glance, still smiling faintly.

Loretta stood in the doorway. The light was behind her, and her wool dress seemed to glow. Her tense white face was fiercely focused on the children. They stared back, blinking, puzzled, at this fuzzy red thing that had come upon them without a sound.

"Loretta," the old man said in a cautious voice. He was astonished by the possessive look in her eyes. She was completely unaware of his presence. Only the children existed, and he could feel the hot wave of her interest surrounding them.

"Mark," she called to the boy.

Tod seemed temporarily bewildered, but he didn't look at the old man for reassurance.

"Mark," she repeated, "I'm talking to you." She came toward the children, and Mr. McGregor saw that she held Ruthie's doll dangling by her side.

"My name isn't Mark," the boy said in a barely audible voice.

"Haven't I told you time and time again to put your dishes on the drain board?" She stood over him, her head tilted. She made no comment about his strange outfit; Mr. McGregor doubted if she even noticed.

"We forgot," said Tod, backing up a step.

"And you, Ruthie," Loretta said, facing the little girl. She held the doll up by one of its limp cloth arms. "You left this on the sofa again. Where did I tell you to put it?"

The girl looked at her brother for help.

"Don't pretend you haven't heard me. Where did I tell

183

you to put it when you're finished playing?"

"Your room," the old man prompted in a whisper. He realized that he should have prepared the children, given them some warning.

"I'm waiting for an answer," Loretta said. Her tone was not angry, only businesslike, impartial.

"My room," said Amy.

"That's right. I want you to take it there." She held out the doll again.

Amy clenched her hands into tiny fists. "No," she said.

Loretta's face went pale. "I won't have you disobeying me. Take your doll to your room."

"Uh-uh."

"She's tired," the old man interjected quickly. "She's been playing all morning. Why don't we make ourselves some coffee in the kitchen?"

Loretta ignored him. "Ruthie! Did you hear what I said?"

"I'm *not* going to my room." Amy glared at her through the slits of her half-closed eyes.

Loretta's self-confidence had begun to waver. She threw the doll to the floor. "You'll listen to your mother!" she cried. "Go to your room this instant."

Tod spoke up, his voice clear and even. "You're not our mother," he said.

Loretta whirled on him, her face showing patches of red. Her eyes had dilated. *"What did you say?"*

The old man stepped between them. "Tod," he shouted, "take your sister and go outside!"

The boy shook his head from side to side. "Uh-uh."

Amy suddenly shrieked, "You're not our mother."

Loretta cringed, and Mr. McGregor put his arm around her, holding her as tightly as he could. "Stop it!" he shouted.

But Amy began to dance around them like a marionette. She seemed to be working herself into a frenzy, spinning across the room until her nurse's cap fell down over her nose. Tod hadn't moved. His finger came up slowly and pointed at Loretta. "Who is she?" he asked.

Alarmed, Mr. McGregor felt he had to protect her from the pointing finger. She had turned away trembling, and he rubbed his hand desperately over her back, stroking, soothing. Amy came up and tried to squeeze between them, but he swept her angrily aside. Then, surprised, he was aware of tears stinging his neck. "Loretta, please," he whispered. "Don't cry. There's nothing to cry about."

There was a sudden sharp expression of pain on her face, and he realized with horror that the boy had pressed his gun into the small of her back. "Damn you!" he exploded.

Tod danced away, waving the weapon. Amy sat down dizzily, exhausted, her face as red as if she had been slapped. ". . . not our mother," she muttered.

Mr. McGregor released his daughter and strode blindly across the room. "Do you see what you've done?" he raged. "I'll teach you." He tore the shoestring from around his neck and lunged toward the sea chest. He unlocked the padlock with the key, took Loretta by the hand, and guided her toward the cabin door. Her body had no driving power of its own; only his fingers, pulling her gently forward, seemed to give her motion.

"Where are they going?" Amy asked Tod.

"You're both being punished," said Mr. McGregor. "Do you understand? Stay here and think about the way you've behaved."

He slammed the cabin door, slipped the padlock through the latch, and secured it firmly from the outside. Tod's face immediately appeared at a porthole. He breathed a film of mist on the glass.

The old man led Loretta across the lawn. He welcomed the dark hallway, the cool, enveloping mustiness of the house. He helped her to climb the steps, one at a time, urging her up with soft whispers. "Don't cry," he crooned. "Please, baby. You'll be fine."

He had closed the blackout curtains in his bedroom and buried the loud ticking alarm clock under a mountain of stockings in his bureau drawer. Loretta lay on the bed, her face against the pillow. She hadn't moved.

Mr. McGregor lowered himself into a chair. It was impossible to think. Everything was in splinters: Amy's moving face, the feel of tears on his neck, the screams of the children, the searing orange and red images in his dream. He stared through the warm darkness at his daughter, hoping that her rest would nourish her. After a while he got up and went to the bed. "Are you all right?" he asked.

Her eyes opened and looked at him. They were no more reassuring than the eyes of the fish in the aquarium.

"See if you can sleep," he said, kissing her lightly on the temple. "I'll drive you back soon." He pressed his hand down over her forehead and her eyes closed, but he could sense that she was still awake. "I'll get you some coffee," he said.

He went out in the hallway and closed the door. Then he turned and started to tiptoe toward the steps.

Loretta cried out, a short scream that was muffled by the pillow.

He hurried back into the room. "What is it?"

Her hands were pressed tightly against her ears. "Voices," she said. "I don't want to hear...." She twisted on the bed, her legs pushing deep folds in the blanket.

"You've been dreaming," he said. He sat down beside her and waited, his fingertips keeping contact with her arm.

Eventually she seemed to relax; her breathing became steady. "Rest," he said. "I'll be right back." The sun had found a crack in the curtains and lay across her back like a trail of spilled flour. "Rest," he repeated, going out into the hall.

He moved toward the stairway again. Where were the lights in the hall? Why were there never any lights? He was on the verge of descending when he heard something from the other wing. Billy?

He retraced his steps. Billy's door stood open and from inside came a muted rustling. He went in.

The two children were crouched at the speaking tube that connected with his bedroom. Tod was whispering into it, blowing, tapping his nails against the metal mouth. The old man watched, appalled. Now it was Amy's turn. She took the tube solemnly and made weird moaning sounds like the wind in the attic.

"Stop that!" he cried out.

Tod saw him and darted away around the edge of the bed. Enraged, the old man moved heavily after him. Amy remained on the floor, blithely biting her thumb.

"Don't you run from me!" he shouted at the boy. "Come here."

"No."

Mr. McGregor lumbered around the bed. "Damn you. How did you get out of the playhouse? What were you doing with that tube?"

"We weren't doing anything." Tod stayed just out of reach.

Short of breath, his heart drumming, the old man kept moving forward. He knew what they had done; they had probably squeezed through a porthole and crept into the house. Then they had thought it a fine joke to frighten Loretta. "Picking on my daughter," he muttered. "I'll teach you to play tricks."

187

"Where's the lady?" Amy asked.

"Forget her!" the old man shouted. "You've done enough damage already." He reached out for Tod. Don't let me hurt him, he prayed.

Frightened, the boy slipped under his arm and bounded across the room toward the door. He pulled violently on the knob. Mr. McGregor, moving faster than he thought was possible, lashed out and caught him around the waist. "I'll teach you," he sang with fury. He brought down his open palm and struck Tod across the face.

"Go away, go away!" the boy screamed.

He struck again. Where was his strap? The old leather one he used for his straight razor and Mark's bottom?

The boy squirmed from his grasp, scampered out of the way, and hid behind his sister. Mr. McGregor stared at him, gulping in air. There was a great crick in his chest; he felt as if he had run a hundred flights of stairs. "Do you want some more?" he said. "Do you want me to get my strap?"

"Go away," said the boy.

The old man breathed deeply, opening and closing his hands. The room was stuffy; perhaps he should open a window. For an instant everything seemed to waver, the ceiling tilting, the furniture elongating like strands of taffy. Then he was all right again. He suddenly remembered he was in the chauffeur's room. "Where's Billy?" he asked.

"We don't know," said Amy.

His anger began to rise again. "I asked you where he is."

Tod climbed up on the bed and sat down with his legs crossed. He reminded the old man of an Indian fakir he had seen in someone's home movies. "He went home."

"Home? What kind of answer is that?" They were obviously still playing with him. "Do you want your supper? Or do you want to stay here till tomorrow morning?"

"We told you," said Tod. "He's not coming back."

It occurred to Mr. McGregor that the boy was telling the truth. Billy, driven by some personal whim, had actually gone for good. No goodbyes, no note—it was typical of him. And it really didn't matter. There was little he could salvage at this point.

"Is the lady going to stay?" Amy asked.

He studied her turned up. "Why? Do you want her to?"

"I don't know."

"Come with me," he said. "Both of you."

"Are you going to hit us with your strap?" Amy asked.

"Not if you do as I say." He led them down the hallway to their room and waved them inside. "Stay here. And *don't* come out."

"Will you bring me my doll?" said Amy.

"Play with your puzzles."

Tod yawned. "Where are you going?"

He didn't answer. He shut the door on them, his anger gone. Poor Loretta. He shouldn't have left her alone.

She still lay on the bed, picking with a bright nail in the soft crook of her arm.

"Don't," he said, trying to take her hand away.

She kept at it. It was bleeding very slightly, like Amy's elbow on the day of the picnic. The old man glanced around the room in despair. "Do you feel any better?" he asked. He had opened the windows but the light was dreary now, almost a winter gray. "Look at the fish," he said. "I find them very relaxing."

The nail picked deeper.

"Won't you talk to me, Loretta?"

She bent the upper half of her body forward, as if she was experiencing a sharp stomach pain.

"I'll take you back," he said softly. "But I've been

thinking. . . . Suppose we try it again next week? The children—"

She screamed. Her fist came to her mouth, and she bit at her knuckles so that the shrieks came through her fingers like terrible whistles.

He drew her to him, folding her in his arms, repeating, "Don't, Loretta, don't. . . ."

She was trembling violently. She bent double again, writhing, and then she was quiet. He kept hugging her, feeling her sweat rub off against his cheek. Her face was so white. Didn't they ever take her out in the sun?

He wouldn't mention the children; he would never mention them again. I didn't mean to hurt you, he thought. I just didn't know, I had no way of telling. "I'm old, Loretta," he said aloud. The sound of his voice startled her. "I'm old," he said again, wiping the perspiration from her face. "I wanted to give you something."

"I have to go back," she said. Her voice was hoarse.

"Yes. All right."

He helped her off the bed and led her to the door, one arm around her shoulder. The house was perfectly still. Stay in your room, he warned the children silently. Don't come out.

They went slowly down the stairway, Loretta clinging to the banister. He could still remember the sound of her screams, their stridency. It had never occurred to him that the children would frighten her and make her worse.

At the foot of the steps she hesitated as Skipper ran in from the kitchen and sniffed around her feet. "This way," the old man said, opening the front door.

They walked to the car through the quickly fading light. He felt gripped by a heavy resignation. He had been asking for too much, expecting the impossible.

Sitting in the car with his daughter huddled beside him, he looked up at the old house. Hundreds of leaves threw their shadows on its walls, a great wave that billowed like smoke. What would he do with the children? He could see them playing endlessly in the playhouse, their hair turning white, their movements restricted by age. Take them back to their mother? No, impossible. But he couldn't keep them. He didn't want to keep them. They had failed him. Tod with his silent mocking face, Amy giggling and confiding to her doll, Ruthie's doll. What could he do with them?

He started the motor and gripped Loretta's hand. "Are you feeling any better?"

Her eyes were on the dashboard, her fingers picking in the hollow of her arm.

"I'm sorry," he said.

The television screen glowed. They were presenting some kind of special news program, loud with throngs of people and chattering announcers.

Mr. McGregor sat in the living room, hardly looking at the set. A TV dinner stood before him on the coffee table, its silver tray congealed with gravy and whipped potatoes. He wasn't hungry, and the sight of the cold food made his stomach heave. It was after nine and dark, but he lacked the energy to close the curtains.

He sat for a long time without moving. Nothing seemed worth the effort, not even checking on the children. They had been docile since his return, eating their TV dinners on the floor of their bedroom. Now there was a great hush from the upper reaches of the house and even Skipper had disappeared.

The set still crackled idiotically, shifting to scenes in various parts of the city. Little black and gray figures scurried back and forth, inky images that flickered on the periphery of his vision. Should he turn it off and go to bed?

No, tonight sleep must be avoided as long as possible, bargained with. He was afraid of its strange hallways and small rooms, its jungle gyms that snapped open and closed like nutcrackers.

". . . the program regularly scheduled for this time has been cancelled," a voice announced from the set.

The old man was puzzled. Program cancelled? That was only done in a period of emergency. Leaning forward, he moved the tray aside and concentrated on the screen. Cameras were trained on the lobby of a Beverly Hills hotel. It was crowded with people under glittering chandeliers. Newcomers kept arriving, men and women loaded down with possessions and carrying small dogs and children.

"More evacuees," the announcer was saying. "Some are carrying all they could salvage on such short notice."

What's going on? Mr. McGregor wondered. It was almost like newspaper photographs from the war years. He felt like shaking the set to clarify it.

The scene shifted abruptly to a wooded hillside. The camera scanned a vast area of ground, hollowed and moonstruck like part of another planet. Dozens of firemen were at work, dragging hoses and equipment across the ground. Trucks and other vehicles loomed up behind them. The old man watched tensely as a commentator approached an official in a strange rubber hat.

"Would you say it's out of control?" the TV man asked.

"Seems that way," the other man admitted. Nearby, in silhouette, a huge roll of hose was being unwound.

"Any possibility it might spread through residential areas?"

The man in the strange hat was grave. "It already has, up Brentwood way. We've dispatched ten engines, but these canyon fires are hard to contain."

"How many homes might be involved?"

"Hard to say, Jerry. We've lost some already."

Good Lord, the old man thought. A fire blowing down

through the canyons, driving whole neighborhoods away. He remembered the police cars he had passed on his way to the sanitarium. And the darkening sky. A fire! He had thought it was only a storm brewing. When had there been a rainfall, moisture on the ground? Not for months. The land was dry as straw.

"We've just received a bulletin," the commentator was saying. "The police and fire departments are asking some of the residents of Bel-Air and Brentwood to evacuate their homes. So far this only applies—repeat—only applies from the southern boundary of Tigertail Road in Brentwood to...."

Mr. McGregor's mouth fell open. He watched, fascinated, as another man told the television audience that the fire department would need all the water it could get. "Tonight's not the time to take a shower or do the dishes."

The old man crossed to the window and looked out. The sky and the lawns were black, peaceful. How far away was it? Close by or miles from the house? Perhaps he should call the local police department. No, better to get the information from the set.

The scene had returned to the hotel lobby. Another newsman was interviewing a high-strung woman who was clutching a French Empire clock and railing against the fire. Terrible, the old man thought. People turned out of their homes with only the clothes on their backs. And yet, though he resisted the idea, it all had an element of farce. Here, instead of the poor, huddled together in some Red Cross tent, was a lobbyful of opulent refugees. They stood, bewildered and petulant, under the glittering chandeliers. He imagined there were film stars among them, and millionaires; perhaps some had even been dining majestically when the fire struck.

The sight of a child sobered him. The little boy was obviously lost and looking for his mother. He cried silently as he pushed his way through the lanes of mink.

Mr. McGregor went to the bar and poured himself a few fingers of brandy. He stoked the logs and built a small fire. For some reason he felt better. The memory of the afternoon was bad enough, but here was something demonstrably worse, a natural catastrophe that could affect hundreds of people.

He settled back on the sofa and kicked off his shoes. Now they were showing the fire from a great distance, a rim of black hill barely lit by flames. He found himself remembering a fire from his youth. A barn had burned down, and he and his friends had watched the horse-drawn bucket brigade arrive in their nightshirts. It had been successfully contained, and they had all stood around later on the farmer's porch lifting cups of cider to their sooty faces.

He watched the set until he lost track of the time. The Swiss clock chimed, but he was too engrossed to count the strokes. Yawning, he wondered if the children had gone to bed—there hadn't been a sound from upstairs. His appetite had mysteriously returned, and he would have liked a sandwich, but he was too tired to go and make it. Sleep had begun to swim in his eyes. What have you planned for me tonight? he wondered. Something special?

Finally he got to hs feet, slid the fire screen in front of the logs, and snapped off the set. Tomorrow he would read about the blaze in the paper, how dozens of valiant men had fought it to a standstill. He didn't want to think about the morning. What was he going to do with the children?

He moved slowly up the stairway. It was very dark; the light over the landing must have burned out. Where could he buy new bulbs? The supermarket, the hardware store?

He had almost reached the second floor when his foot caught in something. Panicking, feeling empty air at his back, he shot out his hands. They missed the banister and the lunge threw him off balance. He tottered, then fell. For a slow-motion moment he seemed suspended, then the hard steps drove themselves into his back, one after another, until he crashed to the floor at the foot of the stairway. He lay there as helpless as a turtle, unable to turn over or even move. Something slithered down beside him—he could see it hit the carpet in the pale firelight from the living room. Loretta's old umbrella, the one with the cat's head for a handle. The last time he had seen it was in the basement. How did it get on the stairway? He was pondering this question when an enormous pain billowed through his body, and he drifted with it into unconsciousness.

Someone was looking at him. He was propped against a tree, listening to the sounds of the ball game, a breeze fanning his face from the lake. There was the little girl watching him, a nymph among the bushes. Go away, he thought. I have a pain in my leg.

He opened his eyes. The hall was filled with a green, almost artificial light. Tod and Amy were standing at the bottom of the stairway. He blinked at them. They were still wearing their costumes which were creased and wrinkled as if they had worn them to bed. "Help me up," he mumbled, his tongue a fat worm. The pain ran the length of his body and found its focus in his right ankle. He gritted his teeth against it.

Amy's voice seemed to come from the attic. "What happened to you?"

". . . tripped." He moved and his arm brushed the curved handle of the umbrella. "Help me."

The children gathered around him, offering their shoulders for support. But he was too heavy. He managed to get to his knees and start crawling toward the living room, clutching at their hands whenever dizziness and nausea threatened to overcome him. The fire had burned out, and there was the Christmas smell of balsam logs. For a spinning moment he thought he was back at the picnic. The ball had hit him, and he lay on the grass with ants in his mouth. Soon Norman would work his way through the crowd.

No. He was in the living room. Straining, he heaved himself up on the sofa and lay there sweating, the pain hammering at his ankle. "Blanket," he murmured.

"What?" said Amy.

"Blanket. My room."

There was whispering, and then he heard someone going up the stairs. He thought of the umbrella. He closed his eyes and saw it walking on little cat's legs up the steps from the basement.

Something rough and woolly brushed his face: the blanket. "Thank you," he said weakly.

"What's wrong with your foot?" Amy? No, deeper. The boy.

"Broken."

"Let's see."

"Don't," he cried out. "Don't touch it."

But the blanket flapped in his face again, and he felt sharp little sticks—fingers?—probing his ankle.

"It's all swelled up," Amy said.

"Get your kit," Tod told her.

"Kit?" he mumbled. "What kit?" He tried to rise on the sofa, but the ceiling wavered over him like a vast moving cloud. He wanted to sleep.

Whispering. Little garter snakes talking. He saw the girl opening the plastic medical kit that had come with her costume. She removed a roll of gauze.

Instinctively, he moved his leg beneath him. "What are you going to do?"

"You have to be bandaged," said Tod.

"I don't want to be bandaged."

Amy bent over him with a toy thermometer in her hand.

196

"You're my patient," she said. "Please open your mouth."

The old man turned away. He could feel the boy's fingers on his foot, the edge of the gauze being looped through his toes. Why argue? he thought, succumbing to a great weariness. They're teasing me. "Are you finished?" he asked the boy.

"Hold still."

"Open your mouth," said Amy.

The foot was now bandaged tightly, almost too tightly, and Tod appeared to be admiring his work with satisfaction.

"He won't let me take his temperature," Amy announced.

"Stop this nonsense," the old man said. "I want to rest."

"We'll take it later," said Tod confidently.

Mr. McGregor pressed his face into the cushions. Why had Billy gone away? He needed him. He dozed on and off, and then he was aware that someone was tickling the bottom of his swollen foot. "Stop it," he cried, drawing his leg up under him.

Tod's face grinned down at him. "Don't you want breakfast?"

"I want a doctor." Something disturbed him. The living room was still dark, though he was sure it was the middle of the morning. The light was a strange underwater color, as if he were floating in his aquarium. "Is is raining out there?" he asked.

"No."

"Why is it so dark?"

Tod didn't seem interested. "You going to sleep again?"

He tried to put some strength in his voice. "I want you to call my doctor. His name is—" what was his name?— "Winston. Dr. Winston. You can look him up in the card file next to the phone in the hallway."

"Aren't you hungry?"

"I'll have some tea later."

"There isn't any."

The old man squirmed with frustration. "Please make that call."

Tod left the room. Where had he gone? Upstairs to whisper with his sister? Then there was a tiny click from the hallway and the sound of the phone being dialed. "Tod?" he called. "Tell him to come over right away."

The boy began speaking very softly to someone. Mr. McGregor strained, but he couldn't make out the words. Skipper started barking in the kitchen, and when he stopped the boy was still talking in a low monotone. Then the receiver dropped back on its hook. The old man permitted himself to relax. What would he tell the doctor about the children, how would he explain their presence? Well, he'd think of something. The important thing was to have his leg attended to. "What did he say?" he called. "When is he coming?"

Tod appeared under the archway. "Later."

"Didn't you tell him it was an emergency?"

"He said he'd try to make is as soon as he can."

The old man sank back on the cushions. Children and doctors. They were so indifferent, so undependable. "You'll have to run down and unlock the gate," he told the boy, reaching inside his shirt for the shoestring. "If it's locked, he'll probably drive away." Where was the string? Had it come loose during his fall, dropped down inside his underwear?

The boy watched him while he searched. Amy joined him under the arch.

It was gone. The shoestring with its two keys, one that opened the gate, the other that fit the padlock on the sea chest in the playhouse. He hadn't removed it in over a year; it was as much a part of him as the little gold wedding band on his finger. "I must have dropped them," he said. "Look on the stairs."

"Dropped what?" said Tod.

"My keys. Check around the stairs. They're important."

The children disappeared, and he could hear their scampering footsteps on the staircase. When they came back they were empty-handed.

"They're not there," said Tod. He ambled to the television set and turned it on. "What time's the cartoon show?"

The little girl sat down on the edge of the sofa. "I think it's over."

Mr. McGregor tried to hoist himself into a sitting position. His ankle throbbed but he succeeded in propping himself on one elbow. The keys. He felt along the cracks between the cushions. Nothing but an old quarter and some cookie crumbs.

The television screen wavered milkily. He could see the shimmering picture past the boy's leaning body. What was this—the fire was still burning? There was a series of high, trembling camera shots, probably taken from a helicopter, of a site of blazing homes, their roofs capped with flames.

"See if it's on channel two," Amy said.

The boy switched. The new channel showed a crowd surging at the mouth of one of the canyons. Policemen were standing guard behind a barrier of wooden sawhorses. That canyon seems familiar, the old man thought. He wrestled with geography for a moment. Was it nearby or miles away?

"Isn't it usually on two?" the boy asked.

"I guess we missed it." The little girl seemed fascinated by the crowd. "Look at all the people."

"It's a fire," Mr. McGregor said. "It might be near here. That's why the sky is so dark."

The boy's face turned toward him with sudden interest. "How do you know?" he asked.

"I was watching it last night on television. Hundreds of people are being evacuated."

Tod grunted. "Maybe I can see it from the roof."

The pain seized his leg, and he grabbed it tightly with

both hands. "Brandy," he gasped. "Get me some brandy."

Amy went behind the bar and returned with a squat decanter. "See?" she said like a scolding parent. "You should have let me take your temperature."

The boy tugged her arm. "Let's go upstairs. Maybe we can see the fire."

They raced out of the room and went scrambling up the steps. Skipper appeared, excited, and barked his way after them. The old man raised the decanter and drank deeply. It didn't contain enough to neutralize the harsh pulsing in his leg; perhaps he should take five or six aspirins with the alcohol.

Time slipped by. He might have been alone at night now; the light had changed to a slate-gray. He had the queer feeling that the woods had grown closer to the house, locking him in with ropey vines and rings of vegetation. If he opened the door branches would poke at his eyes. Everything in the room shone with a luminous quality, the silver lighter on the table, the blue-and-white Wedgwood plates in the breakfront—maybe the pain had polished his senses. He wanted to see the sky. Was it growing black and curly at the edges like a piece of burning paper?

Something thumped on the roof. An awkward bird, the children? He had never been out on the roof. He remembered looking at it only only once from an attic window: a creosote sea sending up blue sheets of heat on a hot summer day. He pictured the children there now, their feet sliding, sticking, as if caught in a pool of molasses.

He drained the decanter and let it bump on the floor. What was wrong with the doctor? Why didn't he come?

More sounds from the ceiling. Maybe they would fall! He pressed his head into the sofa, trying to shut out the thought. Falling. Falling children in his dreams. It wasn't a jungle gym at all. It was his own house with armies of schoolchildren climbing up the shutters, strutting on the roof. His nose twitched in the dusty cushions. He sneezed. Then he slept.

A table was set before him, a funny table. Three porcelain plates, silver service, cut-crystal glasses from his wife's collection, snowy napkins, and three cupcakes with miniature white candles jabbed into their frosty tops.

His eyes fluttered painfully. Tod and Amy were seated at the table. They had doffed their costumes and changed into party clothes. The boy was dressed in his new brown suit, his hair wet from combing. He wore his new tie too, a very nice tie with blue bulldogs on a gray background. The girl was a shimmer of ivory, a cotton dress, cascades of ruffles, a big white bow like a butterfly in her hair. He enjoyed looking at her. She was soothing, the color of clouds.

"What have we here?" he asked, rubbing his face. He felt an urge to scold them for some reason, but it quickly abated.

"We're having my birthday party," the boy said.

"Party?" He wondered if they could hear him. He could hardly hear himself.

"Tod's birthday party," said Amy, smoothing a napkin over her dress.

He tried to fathom what she was talking about. The boy's birthday party. Why hadn't they given him warning? There wasn't any time now to arrange for proper presents. His leg was throbbing, and he hid it under the blanket. No reason to spoil their pleasure because he wasn't feeling well.

Tod lit the candles on each of the cakes with the silver lighter. "We're going to sing 'Happy Birthday' now," he said.

"Fine, fine." Mr. McGregor began to sing as the candles burned, watching the little drops of wax roll down to the plates like pearls. "... Happy birthday, dear To-od..." He noticed that the children weren't singing along with him. They were staring at him, smothering smiles behind their napkins. He broke off sheepishly. "Don't you like my voice? Mark used to tell me it sounded like a bullfrog."

A car horn honked. The old man looked toward the window. It seemed close by, its echo bouncing in the trees. Sternly, with great effort, he tried to collect his scattered thoughts. There *had* been a horn—yes, there it was, sounding again. But who? Dr. Winston! Yes, it was his doctor, parked at the closed gates. "You've got to find the key!" he cried out to Tod.

The boy was licking the icing from his cupcake.

"Didn't you hear that horn? The doctor's here. Find the key and open the gate."

Tod nodded absently and pulled his napkin from his shirt. He placed it carefully on his chair and went out through the archway. The old man lay still, listening as the front door slammed. The boy was an idiot. How did he expect to open the gates without a key?

Amy was stuffing her cupcake into her mouth, the icing oozing through her fingers. "Maybe it's not the doctor," she said.

"Who else would it be?" he asked. But her remark set him to speculating. Was it Norman? Or was it Stauderman, coming to ask angry questions about Loretta?

"Tod didn't call the doctor," she said, primly dabbing her mouth with her napkin.

"Tod didn't—" His voice trailed off. What on earth was she talking about?

"Are you sure you don't want your cake? I've still got plenty of room."

"Of course it's the doctor, Amy."

"Uh huh. Tod only pretended."

"Pretended? Pretended to call the doctor?"

"Uh-huh."

He tried to take her arm. "How do you know?"

"Because I know," she trilled, moving away from him.

"Nonsense," he said. "Help me over to the window." Using both hands he swung his legs off the sofa and planted his feet on the floor. "Come on, now, help me." It was impossible to take any weight on his right foot. He would have to hop or crawl. But as soon as he left the sofa he fell, grabbing the table and pulling down the cloth. The plates clattered to the floor, rolling and spinning like soup tureens. "Give me your arm."

She approached, and he gripped her around the waist. It wasn't far to the window, and he moved, guided by the little girl, a few inches at a time. His right leg seemed paralyzed now; it reminded him of the nights when he had woken in bed full of panic, his arm or leg gone dead, asleep, and he had hung the numb member straight down until gravity had filled it with warm blood and a comforting dazzle of pins and needles.

When they reached the window, he forced himself up, thrusting out both hands to catch himself on the frame. The sky was a vast white mixed with black blotches. There seemed to be flocks of birds hovering over the house, or were they charred remnants from the fire, pieces of smoke?

A police squad car was parked outside the gates and two officers, their shirts blue-black, were talking to Tod. The little boy stood just inside the iron fence, and he nodded as one of them gestured toward the house, then pointed at the horizon.

Policemen and birds. A bad sign, Mr. McGregor thought. He suddenly wanted to laugh, but he fought down the urge. Why had they come in their shiny squad car? For the children? Take them. Take them back to their school or their mother. Perhaps Tod would bring them up to the house for a cup of tea and a piece of cake.

Now the men were leaving. Amy stood next to him watching them back away, her fingers cupped in half-circles against the windowpane. Tod waited until the car had vanished over the brink of the hill, and then he came running toward the house.

Mr. McGregor felt himself slipping gradually to the floor. It was ridiculous, he knew, to let himself just fall, but he was unable to exercise any control. It was almost as if he and his body had parted company. He sat down on the carpet, his legs folding under him at an impossible angle. There was no longer any pain. He was light-headed, almost giddy. He would have liked his cupcake now; he imagined the rich chocolate taste on his tongue.

He could feel a draft as the front door opened. Tod hurried in, out of breath, looking around the room as if he had wandered into the wrong house by mistake.

Mr. McGregor tried to summon his forces, but he found to his dismay that he was yawning. "What did the policeman want?" he asked, surprised by his indifference.

The boy caught his breath. "The fire's coming."

"Fire? Oh, yes—the one on television." Mr. McGregor was hiccuping now, deep spasms rising from his chest. He felt very foolish.

"They want us to leave," Tod told his sister.

She plopped down on the sofa. "I don't want to."

"No, we really have to go."

"Poo." She folded her arms in a parody of annoyance, but the little boy began yanking her arm.

Silly, the old man thought, stifling another yawn. Why couldn't they finish their party?

Whispering. The boy's mouth floating over his sister's ear. Secrets shared with a seashell. Amy pushed him away. "I won't go unless I can take Sam and Sparkle."

The boy relented. "Okay, go get the bowl."

The girl stamped out of the room, and Mr. McGregor sank back on the carpet. He wanted to doze again but the boy's shadow fell over him. "You have to get up."

"Why?" he replied, yawning.

"Because."

The old man shook his head with great resignation and once more tried to rise. Tod pushed at him, helping him. He felt as if he was being erected like a building, floor after floor. Finally he was balancing precariously on his feet. Where were they going? Who would clear up the dishes and the cake crumbs?

"Come on," the boy said, tugging at him with irritation.

Here was Amy again. Amy with a big blue bubble under her arm. Someone's fingers were inside the bubble looking out at him. Then they were moving down the hallway, very slowly. His legs felt like a pair of rusty scissors in an old sewing basket. Rusty scissors with one blade missing.

A bell went off in the house. Were the police coming back? Warm the tea, get two more chairs for the table.

Mr. McGregor swayed against the wall. Through a corridor of wool he could hear Tod far, far away at the end of the hallway. Tod on the telephone. "No," the boy was saying. "Uh-uh, you have the wrong number." The receiver crashed down.

"Why . . ." he managed to say.

Tod shrugged. "Somebody named Norman. Wrong number."

Norman? Yes, Norman. A shame. Norman should have been invited to their party. An oversight. Now he would be angry. He would ride all over the estate in his little sportscar and tear the playhouse down, shingle by shingle. Naughty Norman. He would have to be sent to his room without dinner.

Through the kitchen, a flash of white tile and worn linoleum. Someone had left the refrigerator door open again. Now they were outside under the black sky, and the old man coughed and wheezed. Something stung his eyes and put a tickle in his throat. The fire. Tod had told him about the fire. If it was so close, why didn't he feel its heat on his face like the hot breath of a dog? Everything still seemed green and growing, the trees, the lawn, the shrubbery. It was like the bottom of his fish tank, a miniature plant world that he could watch for hours.

Yes! There it was. Far past the edge of his estate, past his neighbor and his neighbor's neighbor, far out where the sky touched the canyon, was a vivid glow of red and yellow. Was it only a reflection, or did he actually see the flicker of flames in the solid mass of green? There was certainly smoke, volumes of it. But he didn't hear anything; the air was still, the hush before a rainstorm. Weren't fires supposed to roar and thunder like mountain rapids? Perhaps it was still too far away. He ached to get closer so he could hear the very heart of it. Only then would he know that it was real, not some televised picture in black and white.

Something pulled insistently at his hand. Skipper? No, the children. And then it occurred to him with the impact of a revelation that they were leaving. But he couldn't just go as he was. There were things to take, clothes, slippers, money from the safe. "Pictures," he muttered aloud. "I can't go without my pictures."

"What pictures?" a voice asked.

"In the sea chest. I want them."

Whispering. Air hissing from a puncture in a bicycle tire. What had ever happened to Mark's old two-wheeler? Black and silver with a horn that sounded like a duck.

"Do you really want them?"

"Yes."

Falsetto laughter. What was so damn funny? He would put his foot down; he would refuse to go without them.

Then two pairs of hands began tugging at his sleeve, leading him up the steps to the playhouse. How would they get in? The padlock was still on the door; he had locked it when he pulled Loretta away from their taunts. And the key was gone. It had vanished with his shoestring.

Tod was jiggling with the lock. There in his hand, glinting in the strange dark light, was the key. Where had he found it?

The door swung open. Mr. McGregor caught his breath. It was almost as if he was seeing it for the first time, it was so beautiful. The polished lamps, the brass-studded walls, everything nautical and new.

He felt himself losing his balance again—another slow-motion tumble to the floor. More giggles. Then the door slammed, and the padlock clicked shut. Games, he thought sourly. Silly children and their endless games. Mark and Ruthie had been much more well-behaved. But then, they had been properly raised. All the difference in the world. Environment. Firm but loving parents. All the difference in the world.

He lay for a long time where he had fallen. It seemed to him that it was growing brighter outside. Perhaps the sky was finally clearing, and it would turn into one of those spacious and lovely afternoons. He would take the children for a drive, visit the Farmer's Market with its rows of shops and mynah birds talking in bamboo cages. Or maybe—and his heart billowed with the audacity of the idea—maybe he would buy three train tickets, and they would all go back to Michigan, winding past frozen lakes in a twilight of snowflakes.

He crawled his way to the sea chest. Breathing deeply—why was he so tired?—he took out the pictures and drawings, spreading them with great care on the floor. A circle of Marks and Ruthies. Nice Mark. Pretty Ruthie. Run and play. Run, run and play. But all the eyes in the tinted photos were Norman's eyes. He had never noticed that before. He remembered Norman looking down at him on the road. Inspecting his face and the twisted metal wreckage flung over the asphalt like the innards of a complicated toy. No—no, it hadn't been on the road. Later, later as he lay in the hospital. Norman in the white room looking at him through the weave of ropes that held his poor leg in traction.

Go away, Norman. Go away. He tried to gather up the pictures, but they were slippery, playful, they clung to the floor. The little cabin seemed terribly hot; he was sure it was his imagination. Unbutton collar, loosen tie. When were the children going to return and unlock the door? Weren't they tired of their game by now?

He dropped back on the floor. The portholes were growing brighter and brighter, orange and yellow, great sunflowers of light expanding on the glass. Hoist anchor, Billy. Start the diesels. Take compass readings on the bridge. Clear weather, barometer rising, wind north by northeast. He closed his eyes, a gentle motion like the flutter of butterflies. He could feel the throb of the engines from under the floorboards. Billy was at the wheel, good old Billy in a white sailor's cap. Hot. Still hot. Where was the offshore breeze smelling of brine and beaches?

Down St. Cloud Road they would sail, the captain on his bridge waving to other vessels. It would be a long trip but finally, by nightfall, Mr. McGregor was sure he would see his frozen lakes and burning barns.

Katherine and Larry Seidel sat in their stationwagon, brooding over the line of cars in front of them. They were trapped in the heavy bumper-to-bumper traffic on St. Cloud Road, and they had moved no more than a few feet in a quarter-hour. Kate was chain-smoking. She was a yellow-haired girl wearing slacks and a suede jacket that she had pulled from her closet at the last minute. Her husband, bored, was fiddling with a thicket of expensive cameras and leather lens cases that lay on the seat between them. She suddenly noticed that he was wearing a silly brown Tyrolean hat. That was him all over; he had abandoned a closetful of suits and taken that crazy, sentimental hat. "Do we have enough gas?" she asked.

"Plenty." He aimed one of the cameras at her and clicked the shutter. "Portrait of a woman escaping."

"They could have used you on the *Titanic*."

He reached out and ran his finger along the back of her hand. "Could've been worse," he said.

Horns were honking all along the row. No, she reflected sadly, it *couldn't* have been worse. Larry had remained home from the office, and she had waited anxiously all morning by the television set, hoping for a reprieve, while he went up on the roof with some friends and wetted down the shingles. Then a policeman had come and told them they'd have to evacuate, and she had given him a cup of coffee in the foyer. A brand-new house, still smelling of fresh paint, with little stickers on the windows. And she had had such plans for that living room.

"Thank God we're insured," Larry breathed, squeezing her hand.

"May as well turn off the motor," she said. "We're never going to get out of this log jam."

"Patience, honey, patience."

There was still toast in the toaster in the kitchen. Silly thought. It wouldn't be the first time she had burned their food. She wondered what the house would look like when they drove back up the street in a day or two. Just a charred skeleton, open to the wind, with the chimney still standing and two pieces of black bread jutting brightly from the toaster.

"Look," Larry said, pointing through the windshield.

Two little children were emerging from a hole by a high metal gate, a boy and a girl, their clothes stained with dirt and grass. A dog fumbled at their feet, an old half-blind animal with gray fur. The children approached the edge of the road, brushing at themselves.

"They probably got separated from their parents," Kate said. "See if they're all right."

Larry rolled down the window. "Hey, kids!" he called. "That's right, you two. Come over here."

Sweet Lord, the poor little things, thought Kate, watching as they crossed hesitantly toward the car. The girl was carrying a bowl with some kind of fish floating around inside.

"Where are your folks?" Larry asked, opening the door.

The little boy shrugged. His face was grim, and his eyes were narrowed suspiciously. He had the cutest little suit on, Kate thought. Severely cut, like an old man's. The girl didn't seem frightened or upset; bewildered, maybe, but the honking row of cars was enough to confuse anyone. "Is your house near here?" Kate asked the boy.

"Over there." He waved vaguely.

"You two better come with us," Larry said. "We can take you down the hill to a police station."

The children consulted each other silently, then climbed into the car. The little girl was careful not to drip any water from the bowl.

"Want me to hold that for you, honey?" Kate asked.

The girl hugged the bowl to her chest. "No."

"That your dog?" Larry said to the boy.

His long lashes batted. "Uh-uh."

"Well," said Larry, "we can't take the whole neighborhood." The dog was sniffing around the car, whining and trying to lift a paw up to the door. He waved it away.

"Line's moving," said Kate. The car in front of them

210

had started to inch its way down the hill. Larry closed the door and settled behind the wheel.

He glanced over at the little girl; she had snuggled shyly up to his wife. "Don't worry about a thing," he said. "We'll have you back with your parents as soon as we can."

Kate smoothed the girl's long blonde hair. "What kind of fish do you have?"

"Newts. They haven't been fed since yesterday morning."

"They'll survive," Larry said, smiling at her.

The car gained speed, rolling down the hill behind a Rolls-Royce. Kate found a pack of chewing gum in the glove compartment and offered it to the children. They both politely accepted a piece, and the little girl said in a tiny, pleased voice, "Thank you."

Eventually they passed the blockade and joined the stream of cars on Sunset Boulevard. Behind them smoke ran up the sky like a great black tree with towering branches. Ahead, the streets were bathed in long, gusty shafts of sunlight.

"Do you have power steering?" the little girl asked.

BERKLEY HORROR SHOWCASE

Read Them Alone...
If You Dare!

____ **THE TOMB** by F. Paul Wilson   07295-9/$3.95

____ **THE MEPHISTO WALTZ** by Fred Mustard Stewart
       05343-1/$2.95

____ **SHADOWLAND** by Peter Straub   08207-5/$4.50

____ **THE KEEP** by F. Paul Wilson   07489-7/$3.95

____ **WHISPERS** by Dean R. Koontz   07186-3/$3.95

____ **NIGHT CHILLS** by Dean R. Koontz   07760-8/$3.50

____ **PHANTOMS** by Dean R. Koontz   07993-7/$3.95

Prices may be slightly higher in Canada.

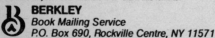